Little Apples

and other
early stories

Little Apples

and other early stories

ANTON CHEKHOV

TRANSLATED BY PETER CONSTANTINE
INTRODUCTION BY CATHY POPKIN

SEVEN STORIES PRESS
NEW YORK • OAKLAND • LONDON

Seven Stories Press
140 Watts Street
New York, NY 10013
www.sevenstories.com

College professors and high school and middle school teachers may order free examination copies of Seven Stories Press. To order, visit www.sevenstories.com or send a fax on school letterhead to (212) 226-1411.

Library of Congress Cataloging-in-Publication Data
Chekhov, Anton Pavlovich, 1860-1904, author.
  [Short stories. Selections. English]
  Little apples and other early stories / Anton Chekhov ; translated by Peter Constantine ; introduction by Cathy Popkin.
     pages ; cm
  ISBN 978-1-60980-664-4 (hardcover)
  ISBN 978-1-60980-768-9 (paperback)
  I. Constantine, Peter, 1963- translator. II. Popkin, Cathy, 1954- writer of introduction. III. Title.
  PG3456.A13C66 2016
  891.73'3--dc23

                                    2015025047

Printed in the United States

9 8 7 6 5 4 3 2 1

Contents

Introduction

by Cathy Popkin

FORTY GOOD READS

Of the nearly six hundred stories collected in *The Complete Works of Anton Pavlovich Chekhov*, more than half stem from Chekhov's early twenties (1880–85), well before he had been embraced by the literary establishment or acclaimed by critics as a great writer.

These were impecunious years for the young Chekhov, who, unlike his illustrious predecessors Tolstoy, Dostoevsky, Turgenev, and Pushkin, emphatically did not hail from aristocracy. The grandson of a serf and the son of a merchant—a bankrupt one at that—the teenage Chekhov had been left behind in his native Taganrog to finish high school and fend off disgruntled creditors while his family fled in the dead of night. When Chekhov arrived in Moscow to matriculate at the university in 1879, he was reunited with parents and five siblings and assumed primary responsibility for the family's keep; a good many of his early stories were written chiefly to keep the Chekhovs housed, clothed, and fed. Studying medicine by day and poring over the popular press after hours, Chekhov published humorous stories and sketches in the comic papers under dozens of pseudonyms; these pieces tended to be short, subject as they were to strict journalistic line limits, and calculated for quick laughs—as well as prompt payment.

Why should we bother, then, with such profit-driven juvenilia? Certainly publishers in the US and UK have shown scant interest in Chekhov's early work. Until relatively recently, only a fraction of the 340-plus stories written before 1886 had appeared in English at all, and fewer still were readily available. Clearly the mythology of the "two Chekhovs"—one a young and callow humorist who dashed off trifles to make ends meet, the other a mature, sober tragedian who produced enduring works of art—has been tough to dislodge; the contrast between some of Chekhov's initial efforts and his later, more widely known work is pronounced. But the connection between the early Chekhov of the comic press and the revered playwright of *The Cherry Orchard* is equally defining; even that last great drama of his Chekhov insisted on calling a comedy.

Indeed, chief among Peter Constantine's purposes in treating us to the zanier side of Chekhov's oeuvre* has been to expand, and especially to diversify, our conception of what counts as "Chekhovian." Not for nothing did Chekhov refer to his own stories as "motley"; until we accommodate the heterogeneity of the parts, we will be missing something essential about the whole.

Nor, importantly, are these variant Chekhovs a consequence of chronology alone. If Chekhov "differed" from himself, that divergence had only partly to do with attaining

---

* Both in the forty stories collected here and in Constantine's earlier collection, *The Undiscovered Chekhov*, published first with thirty-eight new translations and shortly thereafter, in paperback, with forty-three (Seven Stories Press, 1998; 1999).

maturity or changing his modus operandi; Chekhov operated with multiple identities throughout his professional life (even beyond his prodigious use of pseudonyms). As a doctor who was also a writer, a man of science as well as a creator of verbal art, Chekhov actively pursued multiple avenues of investigation from the get-go. In letters to colleagues, he emphasized the complementarity of his disciplines (if I know the theory of circulation *and* can recite poetry, I'm that much richer)* and the synergy of his dual professional allegiances ("when I get tired of one, I spend the night with the other").† During his 1890 research expedition to Sakhalin Island‡ he deployed an especially impressive array of disciplinary approaches. In keeping with the multidisciplinary imperatives of medical geography, Chekhov surveyed the hygienic conditions of the penal colony by collecting the data of an ethnographer, geographer, meteorologist, demographer, cartographer, sociologist, statistician, and physician. Chekhov's literary forays, too, lay bare the possibilities and pitfalls of all kinds of investigatory practices, from diagnosis to deposition, from library to laboratory, from microscopy to metaphysics, from painting to politics.

If Chekhov was attuned to the plurality of possible modes of *reconnaissance* he was equally fascinated by his era's myriad forms of *documentation*, the profusion of specialized formats for recording and disseminating one's professional

---

* To Alexei Suvorin, May 15, 1889.
† The punch line of Chekhov's oft-cited quip, "Medicine is my lawfully wedded wife, literature is my mistress" (to Suvorin, September 11, 1888).
‡ Bleak island in the Sea of Japan, to which Russia exiled thousands of prisoners in the nineteenth century.

findings. From the time he was learning to construct medical case histories at school while also scouring the papers to figure out which literary genres might sell, Chekhov developed an abiding interest in the many possible ways to structure an effective—and affective—account. In the course of his careers both scientific and literary, Chekhov experimented with documentary formats as diverse as statistical tables, exhibition catalogues, obituary notices, census questionnaires, letters, travelogues, timelines, diagrams, photographs, drawings, and diary entries, not to mention the idiosyncratic short stories and innovative dramatic forms he refined to such a level of artistry.

This preoccupation with documentary, expository, and artistic form is arguably the most defining by-product of Chekhov's commitment to more than one line of inquiry. It is surely the hallmark of his best-known work: it conjures up the Akathist Hymn* we long to hear in "Easter Eve" (1886), the psychiatric case history that structures "A Nervous Breakdown" (1889), the Gospel story that both moves and betrays in "The Student" (1895), the error-ridden telegram that brings sad tidings in "The Darling" (1899), the Christmas letter that fails—or, by some miracle, succeeds—in establishing contact "At Christmastime" (1900), the parable (of the prodigal son) that doesn't hold up in "The Bride" (1903), along with the innumerable other verbal artifacts (anecdotes, arias, autopsy reports, calendars, caricatures, equations, laments, lectures, ledgers, legends, math problems, moral exempla, newspaper clippings,

---

* Special canticle with a complicated and highly specified structure.

property assessments, psalms, saints' lives, sermons, songs, syllogisms, transcripts, and a wide variety of liturgical offerings) that underlie Chekhov's work throughout.

It's not hard to spot the documentary forms lurking in the stories of the present volume; they include such verbal specimens as the typology ("The Temperaments—According to the Latest Science"), the feuilleton ("Salon des Variétés"), government regulations ("Persons Entitled to Travel Free of Charge on the Imperial Russian Railways"), down to the minutes of a professional meeting ("The Philadelphia Conference of Natural Scientists"). Some stories actually wear their genres on their sleeves: "An Idyll—But Alas!"; "The Turnip: A Folktale"; "Twenty-six (Excerpts from a Diary)"; "A Brief Anatomy of a Man"; "A Children's Primer"; "On the Characteristics of Nations (From the Notebook of a Naïve Member of the Russian Geographic Society)"; "A Modern Guide to Letter Writing"; "Visiting Cards"; "Letters to the Editor"; "Man (A Few Philosophical Musings)"; and so on.

In many cases, what makes these renditions entertaining is the incompetence with which the paradigm in question is deployed: "Dirty Tragedians and Leprous Playwrights: A Dreadful, Terrible, and Scandalously Foolhardy Tragedy" is self-evidently a script, but one that contains largely words that are *not* meant to be spoken onstage. In other instances the content is grotesquely incongruent with the form that purveys it. When a high-ranking official in "The Eclipse" orders that the street lanterns remain lit throughout the night so that the eclipse of the moon will be visible, and cautions his interlocutors about the subversive potential of such planetary misbehavior, we are amused by his inexorable logic. But what makes the exchange most absurd is the form it takes: a sequence of documents in an official correspondence—Memorandum No. 1032 and its serial responses (Re: Memorandum No. 1032, etc., etc.)—with inflated rhetoric to match and witness signatures to provide authentication.

By exemplifying a recognizable genre or form but violating its norms, lampoons like these confirm in the breach the potency of a culture's forms of writing. Still, we hardly need to know the specifics of nineteenth-century Russian bureaucratic culture to chuckle at Memorandum No. 1032 (etc.); neither is the overexposure of Chekhov's single white male in his 1880 send-up of a personal ad ("À l'américaine") lost on readers familiar with online dating. And the grammatical infelicities in student writing haven't gotten any less impressive since Chekhov's day ("Nadia N.'s Vacation Homework"). These stories are *still* funny.

But Chekhov's interests go beyond poking fun at his contemporaries (and ours!), or even capitalizing on comedy when the cupboards were bare. Moreover, not all of his early stories are humorous, any more than the later ones are uniformly dark.

Perhaps the least funny of this lot is the title tale, "Because of Little Apples"—certainly the characters who do find humor in the state of affairs are the story's most depraved. This latter-day incarnation of the Garden of Eden is already a fallen world, one whose denizens are deeply flawed and whose temptations are legion. There, beneath the tree of knowledge, different forms of cultural literacy are put to the test. Readers of the tale must rise to the epistemological challenges of several *fields*—religion, history, and literature—if they are to make sense of the setting, at once so mythically broad and so historically specific as well as symbolically rich; meanwhile, the boy and girl in the story are being judged on their knowledge of specific *genres*—stories, commandments, and prayers. For the vulnerable pair within the story, the penalty for inadequate mastery will be irrevocable loss.

In his singular attentiveness to fields and forms—the structures of knowledge and modes of communication—Chekhov explores how people attempt to construct meaning, how they make recourse to the categories of their culture, how they harness them and not infrequently become entrapped by them, misappropriating and misapplying such discursive frameworks in botched attempts to make sense of their lives or to communicate their plight. If, as we've noted, the discrepancy between actual situations and the clichéd, overblown, or otherwise inappropriate formulations used to represent them serves as a rich source of humor in Chekhov's tales, this stubborn attachment to narratives or other forms of accounting that simply do not fit the context also has the potential to unleash great suffering. At base, Chekhov is interested in how people understand their predicaments, how they shape their responses and frame their behaviors, how people attempt and all too often fail to comprehend their own pain and, more frequently still, to tap into the pain of others.

In this respect, anyway, Chekhov's capacity to "think medically" never deserted him, even when he was composing fiction. In fact, what aligns the two practices Chekhov was honing in the early 1880s (and what also amply justifies his professional "two-timing") is their common goal of access—clinical and imaginative—to somebody else's pain. Insofar as the stories in this volume illustrate vividly (and often hilariously) the frustrations and failures born of the wide gulf between life and our misguided constructions of it, they do serve a diagnostic function. These stories also have a certain palliative potential: if they don't fully deliver us from evil, they do divert us and lighten thereby our post-lapsarian load. And if by chance we should be edified and thus raised by them, then Chekhov's early comedic tales will have proved therapeutic as well.[*]

---

[*] I am indebted to Paul Reardon for this line of thought ("From Case Study to Comedy: Representation in Chekhov's Early Stories," unpublished).

Translator's Note

Anton Chekhov's short and remarkably productive writing career spanned the last two decades of the nineteenth century. He was forty-four years old when he died in 1904, a man about to reach his prime (though the most lasting image of him has been a photograph from his final years: frail, wizened, and with a walking stick, an elder of Russian literature). From his two decades as a writer, Chekhov's greatest output was when he was in his twenties. It is in this period, the 1880s, that he published some of his best-known comic and tragicomic stories—"Oysters," "The Swedish Match," "The Kiss," "The Steppe"—and his first play, *Ivanov*.

One of the pleasures of translating the Chekhov stories in this edition, works from the first half of his literary career that are lesser-known and even unknown in the English-reading world, is his ever-changing range of styles and story formats, his innovative and unexpected approach. The reader is struck by the creative energy and by Chekhov's take on the absurd: one has to remind oneself that these pieces were written in the 1880s, some thirty years before Futurism, Dada, and other avant-garde writing. Chekhov's comic and tragic timing is masterful, whatever the story's format, whether in the guise of a traditional narrative or the zany forms of a medical prescription, or an administrative directive from the Russian railroads stating that horses, donkeys, and oxen in the service of the railroads are permitted to travel free of charge in second-class compartments. Chekhov's words are arranged for the best theatrical effect. This mastery of timing is part of the dramatic skill that comes to the fore in his plays.

Chekhov has been an elusive author: for over a century people have been trying define what is "Chekhovian." Nabokov's unkind (or perhaps humorous) definition of the word is "dragging, hopelessly complicated." Other definitions have been "bleakly Russian," and "evocative of a mood of introspection and frustration." The aim of this collection is to widen the horizons of what "Chekhovian" means.

I am grateful to the National Endowment of the Arts, the Dorothy and Lewis B. Cullman Center for Scholars and Writers at the New York Public Library, and the Ellen Maria Gorrissen Berlin Prize of the American Academy of Berlin for their generous support of this project. I am also thankful to Burton Pike for his scholarly advice and encouragement.

Little Apples
and other
early stories

BECAUSE OF
LITTLE APPLES

B etween the Black Sea and the White Sea, at a certain longitude and latitude, the landowner Trifon Semyonovich has resided since time out of mind. His family name is as long as the word "Overnumerousnesses," and derives from a sonorous Latin word referring to one of the countless human virtues. He owns eight thousand acres of black earth. His estate—because it is an estate, and he is a landowner— is mortgaged to the hilt and has been foreclosed and put up for sale. The sale was initiated in the days before the first signs of Trifon Semyonovich's bald spot, and has been drawn out all these years. As a result of the bank's credulity and Trifon Semyonovich's resourcefulness, things have been moving very slowly indeed. The bank will one day fail because Trifon Semyonovich and others like him, whose names are legion, have taken the bank's rubles but refuse to pay the interest. In the rare cases that Trifon Semyonovich does make an interest payment, he does so with the piety of an upright man donating a kopeck for the souls of the dead or the building of a church. Were this world not this world, and were we to call things by their real names, Trifon Semyonovich would not be called Trifon Semyonovich but something else; he would be called what a horse or a cow might be called. To put it bluntly, Trifon Semyonovich is a swine. I invite him to challenge this. If my invitation reaches him (he sometimes reads this magazine), I doubt that he will be angry, as he is a man of intelligence. In fact, I'm sure he will agree with me completely, and in the autumn might even send me a dozen Antonov apples from his orchards as a thank-you for only having revealed his Christian name and patronymic, and hence not utterly ruining his lengthy family name. I shall not catalogue Trifon Semyonovich's many virtues: the list is too long. For me to present him—arms, legs, and all—I would have to spend as much time at my desk as Eugène Sue did with his ten-volume *Wandering Jew*. I will not touch upon the tricks Trifon Semyonovich resorts to when playing cards, nor upon his wheeling and dealing, by dint of which he has avoided paying any debts or interest, nor will I list the pranks he plays on the priest and the sexton, nor how he rides through the village in a getup from the era of Cain and Abel. I shall limit myself to describing a single scene that characterizes his attitude toward mankind, an attitude beautifully summed up in the tongue twister he composed, prompted by his seventy-five-year experience of the human race: "Foolish fools fooled foolishly by foolish fools."

One wonderful morning, wonderful in every sense (for the incident occurred in late summer), Trifon Semyonovich was strolling down the long paths and the short paths of his sumptuous orchard. Everything that might inspire a lofty poet lay scattered about in great abundance, and seemed to be saying and singing: "Partake, O man, partake in the bounty! Rejoice while the sweet days of summer last!" But Trifon Semyonovich did not rejoice, for he is not a poet, and that morning his soul, as Pushkin said, "did yearn so keenly for quenching sleep" (which it always did whenever that soul's owner had had a particularly bad evening at cards). Behind Trifon Semyonovich marched his lackey Karpushka, a little man of about sixty, his eyes darting from side to side. Old Karpushka's virtues almost surpass those of Trifon Semyonovich. He is a master at shining boots, even more of a master at hanging stray dogs, spying into other people's business, and stealing anything that isn't nailed down. The village clerk had dubbed him "the Oprichnik,"* which is what the whole village now calls him. Hardly a day passes without the neighbors or the local peasantry complaining to Trifon Semyonovich about Karpushka, but the complaints fall on deaf ears since Karpushka is irreplaceable in his master's household. When Trifon Semyonovich goes for a stroll he always takes faithful Karpushka with him: it is safer that way and much more fun. Karpushka is a fountain of tall tales, jingles, and yarns, and an expert at not being able to hold his tongue. He is always relating this

---

* A member of a sinister private army devoted to the service of Czar Ivan the Terrible.

or that, and only falls silent when something interesting catches his ear. On this particular morning he was walking behind his master, telling him a long tale about how two schoolboys wearing white caps had ridden past the orchard with hunting rifles, and begged him to let them in so they could take a few shots at some birds. They had tried to sway him with a fifty-kopeck coin, but he, knowing full well where his allegiance lay, had indignantly refused the coin and even set Kashtan and Serka loose on the boys. Having ended this story, Karpushka began portraying in vivid colors the shameful behavior of the village medical orderly, but before he could add the finishing touches to this portrayal his ears suddenly caught a suspicious rustle coming from behind some apple and pear trees. Karpushka held his tongue, pricked up his ears, and listened. Certain that this rustle was indeed suspicious, he tugged at his master's jacket, and then shot off toward the trees like an arrow. Trifon Semyonovich, sensing a brouhaha, shuddered with excitement, shuffled his elderly legs, and ran after Karpushka. It was worth the effort.

At the edge of the orchard, beneath an old, gnarled apple tree, stood a young peasant girl, chewing something. A broad-shouldered young man was crawling on his hands and knees nearby, gathering up apples the wind had knocked off the branches. The unripe ones he threw into the bushes, but the ripe apples he lovingly held out to his Dulcinea in his large, dirty hands. It was clear that Dulcinea had no fear for her stomach; she was devouring one apple after another with gusto, while the young man crawled and gathered more and only had eyes for his Dulcinea.

"Get me one from off the tree," the girl urged him in a whisper.

"It's too dangerous."

"Too dangerous? Don't worry about the Oprichnik, he'll be down at the tavern."

The boy got up, jumped in the air, tore an apple off the tree, and handed it to the girl. But the boy and the girl, like Adam and Eve in days of old, did not fare well with this apple. No sooner had she bitten off a little piece and handed it to the boy, and they felt its cruel tartness on their tongues, than their faces blanched, puckered up, and then fell. Not because the apple was sour, but because they saw before them the grim countenance of Trifon Semyonovich, and beside it the gloating face of Karpushka.

"Well hello," Trifon Semyonovich said, walking up to them. "Eating apples, are we? I do hope that I am not disturbing you."

The boy took off his cap and hung his head. The girl began eyeing her apron.

"And how have you been keeping, Grigory?" Trifon Semyonovich said to the boy. "Is everything going well?"

"I only took one," the boy mumbled. "And it was lying on the ground."

"And how have you been keeping, my dear?" Trifon Semyonovich asked the girl.

The girl studied her apron more intensely.

"The two of you not married yet?"

"Not yet, Your Lordship . . . but I swear, we only took one, and it was . . . um . . . lying—"

"I see, I see. Good fellow. Do you know how to read?"

"No . . . but I swear, Your Lordship, it was only one, and it was lying on the ground."

"So you don't know how to read, but you do know how to steal. Well, at least that's something. Knowledge is a heavy burden. And have you been stealing for a long time?"

"But I wasn't stealing."

"What about your sweet little bride here?" Karpushka asked the boy. "Why is she so sad? Don't you love her enough?"

"No more of that, Karpushka!" Trifon Semyonovich snapped. "Well, Grigory, I want you to tell us a story."

The boy cleared his throat nervously and smiled.

"I don't know any stories, Your Lordship," he said. "And it's not like I need your apples. If I want some, I can buy some."

"My dear fellow, I am delighted that you have so much money. Come, tell us a story. I am all ears, Karpushka is all ears, and your pretty little bride is all ears. Don't be shy. Be brave! A thief's heart must be brave! Is that not so, my friend?"

Trifon Semyonovich rested his venomous eyes on the crest-fallen boy. Beads of sweat gathered on the boy's forehead.

"Why don't you tell him to sing a song instead?" Karpushka piped up in his tinny tenor. "You can't expect a fool like that to come up with a story."

"Quiet, Karpushka! Let him tell us a story! Well, go on, my dear fellow."

"I don't know any stories."

"So you can't tell a story, but you can steal. What does the Eighth Commandment say?"

"I don't know, Your Lordship, but I swear we only ate one apple, and it was lying on the ground."

"Tell me a story!"

Karpushka began gathering nettles. The boy knew perfectly well why. Trifon Semyonovich, like all his kind, is a master at taking the law into his own hands. He will lock a thief up in his cellar for a day and a night, or flog him with nettles, or let him go right away—but not before stripping him naked and keeping his clothes. This surprises you? There are people for whom this is as commonplace as an old cart. Grigory peered sheepishly at the nettles, hesitated, cleared his throat, and launched into what was more a tangle of nonsense than anything resembling a story. Gasping, sweating, clearing his throat, blowing his nose, he muttered something about ancient Russian heroes fighting ogres and marrying beautiful maidens. Trifon Semyonovich stood listening, his eyes fixed on the storyteller.

"That'll do," he said when the young man's tale finally fell apart completely. "You are an excellent storyteller, but an even better thief. As for you, my pretty little thing," he said, turning to the girl, "say the Lord's Prayer."

The girl blushed and said the Lord's Prayer, barely audibly and with hardly a breath.

"Now, how about the Eighth Commandment?"

"We didn't take a lot," the boy replied, desperately waving his arms. "I swear by the Holy Cross!"

"It is very bad, my dear children, that you don't know

this commandment. I will have to teach it to you. Tell me, my pretty one, did this fellow teach you how to steal? Why so silent, my little angel? You must answer me. Answer me! You are silent? Your silence means you obviously agree. Since this is the case, my pretty one, you will have to beat your fiancé for having taught you how to steal!"

"I won't," the girl whispered.

"Just a little. Fools must be taught a lesson. Go on, beat him, my pretty one. You won't? Well, in that case I shall have to ask Karpushka and Matvei to give you a little beating with those nettles over there. Shall I?"

"I won't," the girl repeated.

"Karpushka, come over here, will you?"

The girl flew at the boy and slapped him. The boy smiled foolishly and began to cry.

"That was excellent, my dear. Now pull his hair. Go to it, my dear. What, you won't? Karpushka, can you come here, please?"

The girl grabbed her betrothed by the hair.

"Don't hold back, I want it to hurt! Pull harder!"

The girl began pulling. Karpushka bubbled over with delight.

"That will do," Trifon Semyonovich said to the girl. "Thank you for doing your bit to punish evil, my pretty one. And now," he said, turning to the young man, "I want you to teach your fiancée a lesson. I want you to do to her what she has done to you."

"Please, Your Lordship, by God . . . why should I beat her?"

"Why? Didn't she just beat you? Now beat her! It will do her a world of good. You won't? Well, there's nothing for it. Karpushka, go get Matvei, will you?"

The boy spat, gasped, seized his fiancée's braid, and began doing his bit to punish evil. Without realizing it he fell into a trance, got carried away, and forgot that it was not Trifon Semyonovich he was beating, but his betrothed. The girl shrieked. The beating went on for a long time. God knows where it would have ended if Trifon Semyonovich's pretty daughter Sashenka had not appeared through the bushes.

"Papa dear, do come and have some tea!" she called, and seeing her dear papa's little caper, burst into peals of laughter.

"That'll do, you can go now," Trifon Semyonovich said to the girl and boy with a low bow. "Goodbye. I'll send you some nice little apples for your wedding."

The girl and the boy went off—the boy to the right, the girl to the left. From that day on they never met again. Had Sashenka not appeared when she did, they might have been whipped with nettles too. This is how Trifon Semyonovich amuses himself in his old age. And his family isn't far behind. His daughters have a habit of sewing onions onto the hats of guests whom they "outrank socially," and should these outranked guests have had a drink or two too many, the girls take a piece of chalk and write "Donkey" or "Fool" in thick letters on their backs. Last winter, Trifon Semyonovich's son Mitya, a retired lieutenant, even managed to outdo his papa. He and Karpushka smeared the gates of a retired soldier with tar because the soldier wouldn't give Mitya a wolf cub he wanted, and because the soldier had warned his daughters against accepting cakes and candy from the lieutenant.

And after this you want to call Trifon Semyonovich, Trifon Semyonovich and not something worse?

À L'AMÉRICAINE

I, experiencing the urgent whim to enter a thoroughly lawful marriage, and realizing that no marriage can be entered into without a female of the species, have the honor and pleasure of asking all young maidens and widows to cast a favorable eye on the following:

First and foremost, I am a man. Needless to say, this is a point of some importance to the ladies. I stand one yard and twenty-seven inches tall. I am young. Indeed, I am as far from middle age as a flock of sandpipers would be from Novosibirsk on St. Peter's Day. I am of noble lineage. I might not be much to look at, but am not that bad either, so much so that I have been repeatedly mistaken for handsome, albeit only on moonless nights. My eyes are hazel. My cheeks (alas!) are undimpled. Two of my back teeth are rotten. I have a hard time assuming graceful manners, but no one should doubt the strength of my muscles. (My glove size is 7¾.) I have nothing to my

13

name but my poor though wellborn parents. I do, however, have an illustrious future before me. I am a devotee of pretty women in general and parlor maids in particular. I believe in everything. I am a man of letters—so much so that I am above shedding tears when rejection slips come pouring in. I see a novel in my future, whose heroine (a wanton but exquisite beauty) will be modeled on my wife-to-be. I sleep twelve hours a night. I eat mountains of food. I drink vodka only in company. I have a commendable circle of friends: I know two literati, a ditty-writer, and two men about town who have dedicated their lives to the betterment of mankind by writing articles for *The Russian Gazette*. My favorite poets are Pushkarev and, at times, myself. I am amorous, but not in the least jealous. I wish to marry for reasons known only to myself and my creditors. That, in a nutshell, is who I am!

Now as to what I am looking for in a wife. She must be either a maiden or a widow, whichever she prefers, not older than thirty nor younger than fifteen. She must not be Catholic—in other words not one of those women who believe that there is such a thing as a man who is infallible—and definitely not a Jewess. A Jewess would never tire of badgering me: "*Oy*, is that all those magazines are paying you for a line? You should go to my papa and learn one or two things about making rubles!" I would not like that. I would like a blonde with blue eyes and, please, if at all possible, dark eyebrows. She must not be pale, flushed, thin, plump, tall, or squat, but pleasant, and not possessed by demons, or have her hair cut short, or be garrulous, or never want to go anywhere.

She must have good handwriting, because I need some-one to copy out my pieces. Not that there's much to copy out.

She must love the magazines I write for, and follow the mode of life they advocate.

She must not read *The Playful Tattler*, *The New Daily*, or that dreadful book *Nana*, and she should not be moved by the feature articles of *The Moscow News*, or swoon at the poetry that keeps appearing in *Berega*.

She must be able to sing, dance, read, write, boil, roast, fry, be sweet and tender, grill (but without raking me over the coals), be good at borrowing money for her husband, have a knack for dressing elegantly using *her own financial resources* (N.B.!), and be absolutely obedient.

She must not niggle, hiss, squawk, yell, bite, bare her teeth, throw plates, or bat her eyelashes at friends of the family.

It is important that she remember that horns do not adorn a man's head, and that the shorter they are the safer is he who will be made to pay for them.

She must not be called Matryonna, Akulina, Avdoteya, or other such provincial names, but have a nobler name, such as Olya, Lenochka, Maruska, Katya, Lipa.

She must at all times keep her dear mama, my highly esteemed mother-in-law, well away from me, somewhere at the back of beyond, otherwise I cannot be held accountable for my actions, and—

She must have a minimum of two hundred thousand rubles in silver.

This stipulation, however, is negotiable at the discretion of my creditors.

THE
TEMPERAMENTS

(According to the Latest Science)

T*he Sanguine Man*. Impressions work on him easily and quickly. This, according to Hufeland, leads to his being frivolous. In his young years he is a prankster and a ne'er-do-well. He talks back to his teachers, will not cut his hair, does not shave, wears glasses, and scribbles on walls. He is not good in class, but graduates. He is disrespectful to his parents. If he is wealthy, he is a dandy; if poor, he lives in squalor. He sleeps until noon, and goes to bed at all hours. His spelling leaves much to be desired. Nature has made him for love alone; consequently he will only occupy himself with what he loves. He is not above drinking himself to kingdom come. Drinking late into the night until little green devils dance before his eyes, he rises the following day somewhat bedraggled, but with only a slight dullness in his head, and without the urge to *similia similibus curantur.*[*] He marries by mistake, and is forever engaged in battle with his mother-in-law and at war with his wife. He lies to beat the band. He is drawn to brawling and sentimental plays. In an orchestra he is the first violin. Being flighty, he is a liberal. The sanguine man will either read nothing all his life or read himself into oblivion. When it comes to newspapers, he loves editorials and is not above editorializing. The readers' page of humorous magazines was expressly invented for him. He is constant in his inconstancy. In the government, he is an official for special matters or the like. If he is an instructor, he instructs literature. He will rarely work his way up to the rank of state councilor, but if he should reach that highest of ranks in our civil service he turns into a phlegmatic man, sometimes even a choleric one. Freeloaders, crooks, and beer-swillers are sanguine individuals. Sleeping in the same room as the sanguine man is not to be recommended as he will tell jokes all night, and, when he has run out of jokes, will begin criticizing his friends or telling lies. He succumbs to illnesses of the digestive system and premature exhaustion.

The sanguine woman is quite bearable, so long as she is not a fool.

The Choleric Man. He is bilious and sports a sallow complexion. His nose is somewhat crooked, and his eyes circle in their sockets like hungry wolves in cramped cages. He is irritable. Bitten by a flea or pricked by a needle, he is ready

---

[*]　Latin: "cure like with like." [Translator]

to blow the world to kingdom come. Every time he speaks it is with a spray of spittle, and he bares teeth that are either brown or very white. He is convinced that it is always "cold as hell" in winter and "hot as hell" in summer. He hires and fires cooks every week. When he dines, he complains that everything is either overcooked or too salty. Most choleric men are bachelors, but if they do marry they keep their wives under lock and key. He is jealous as the devil. He has no sense of humor, and everything annoys him. He only reads newspapers so he can swear at journalists—when still in his mother's womb, he was already convinced that all newspapers lie. As a husband or friend he is unbearable; as a subordinate, obsequious; as a boss, insufferable and in everyone's way. More often than not, unfortunately, he is a pedagogue, teaching mathematics and ancient Greek. I do not advocate sleeping in the same room with him, as he will cough and spit all night and swear loudly at the fleas. If he hears a hen cackling or a cock crowing in the middle of the night he will clear his throat, and, in a rasping voice, call for his servant to climb onto the roof, seize the creature, and wring its damned neck. He dies of a lung or liver ailment.

The choleric woman is a devil in a dress, a crocodile.

The Phlegmatic Man. A most agreeable individual (needless to say I am not referring to British phlegmatics, but Russian ones). He is quite unremarkable in appearance, and somewhat ungainly. He is always serious, because he is too lazy to laugh. He will eat anything and at any time. He does not drink because he is afraid of fits, and sleeps twenty

hours a day. He sits on every possible committee and is
to be found at every meeting and emergency session but
is at a loss about what is going on, and dozes off without
a twinge of conscience, patiently waiting for the meeting
to end. At the age of thirty, with the assistance of uncles
and aunts, he marries. He is the most suitable person for
marriage: he agrees with everything, never grumbles, and is
completely complacent. He calls his wife "sweetheart." He
loves suckling pig with horseradish, all things sour, choral
music, and the cool shade. The phrase *vanitas vanitatum et
omnia vanitas** (nonsense of nonsenses, and all is nonsense)
was coined with the phlegmatic man in mind. He only falls
ill when he is called upon to serve as a juror. When he sees
a portly woman he wheezes, begins fidgeting, and attempts
to smile. He has a subscription to *Niva*, but is peeved that
they do not color their pictures and have no funny articles.
He considers writers extremely clever, but at the same time
extremely dangerous. He laments that his children are not
whipped at school, but is himself at times not averse to giving them a good hiding. He is happy in the civil service. In
an orchestra he is the contrabass, bassoon, or trombone; in
a theater the cashier, doorman, or prompter—and at times,
pour manger, an actor. He ultimately falls victim to paral-
ysis or dropsy.

The phlegmatic woman is a hefty, pop-eyed, flour-white
German woman of means prone to tears. She calls to mind
a sack of flour. She is born to become a mother-in-law, a
condition toward which she strives.

---

* "Vanity of vanities, all is vanity." [Translator]

The Melancholic Man. Gray-blue eyes, brimming with tears. There are deep lines on his forehead and on either side of his nose. His mouth is somewhat crooked, his teeth black. He inclines to hypochondria, forever complaining of a pain in the pit of his stomach, a stitch in his side, and weak digestion. His favorite pastime is to stand before a mirror eyeing his limp tongue. He believes his lungs are weak and that he is suffering from a nervous condition, and consequently drinks herbal potions instead of tea, and elixir of life instead of vodka. With sorrow and in a faltering voice, he informs those near and dear to him that laurel tinctures and valerian drops are not availing. He feels that it would not be amiss to take a purgative once a week. He long ago decided that doctors do not understand him. Faith healers and healeresses, quacks, drunken field medics, and sometimes midwives give him succor. He dons a heavy winter coat in September and only takes it off in May. He suspects rabies in every dog, and ever since a friend informed him that a cat is capable of suffocating a sleeping man, he sees in every feline an implacable enemy of mankind. He drew up his will long ago. He swears by God and the Holy Bible that he never touches alcohol, but from time to time will imbibe warm beer. He marries a destitute orphan. If he does have a mother-in-law, he idealizes her as the epitome of brilliance and wisdom, listening to her pontifications with rapture, his head tilted to the side. Kissing her plump, clammy hands, redolent of sour pickles, he considers to be the holiest of duties. He pursues an active correspondence with uncles, aunts, his godmother, and childhood friends. He doesn't read newspapers: he used to read *The Moscow Daily*, but as he felt his stomach constricting, his heart racing, and his eyes glazing over, he gave it up. He secretly reads Auguste Debay and Jozan de Saint-André's books on conjugal hygiene. When the plague descended on Vetlyansk he devoutly resolved to fast five times. He is beset by nightmares and fits of weeping. He is not particularly happy in the civil service, and never rises above the rank of a minor section chief. He likes singing the old folk song "Luchinushka." In an orchestra, he is the flute or the violoncello. He sighs night and day, which is why I advise against sleeping in the same room with him. He foretells floods, earthquakes, wars, the moral decline of mankind, and his own death from some agonizing illness. He dies of heart disease, cures administered by faith healers, and often of hypochondria.

The melancholic woman is the most unbearable and fretful of creatures. As a wife, she drives her husband to desperation and suicide. The one good thing is that it is not difficult to get rid of her: give her some money and she will set off on a pilgrimage.

The Choleric-Melancholic Man. In his early years he is a sanguine youth, but the instant a black cat crosses his path or the devil clouts him on the head, he turns into a choleric-melancholic individual. I am speaking of my illustrious Moscow neighbor, the exalted editor of the *Zritel* magazine. Ninety-nine percent of our Slavophile nationalists are choleric-melancholics, as are all unacknowledged poets, *pater patriae*, Jupiters, unacknowledged Demosthenes, and cuckolded husbands. Choleric-melancholic men are all those who are weakest in body but strongest in voice.

SALON DES VARIÉTÉS

"Cabbie! Are you asleep, dammit? Get me to the Salon des Variétés!"

"Um . . . ah . . . the saloon day very tea? That'll be thirty kopecks, sir."

Lit by lanterns: the entrance and a lone constable loitering outside. A ruble and twenty kopecks to get in and twenty kopecks to check your coat (the latter, however, is not mandatory). You barely put your foot inside the door when the potent stench of shoddy boudoirs and bathhouse changing rooms washes over you. The guests are slightly tipsy. Incidentally, I would discourage a visit to the salon by anyone who is—how shall I put it—not at least three, if not four, sheets to the wind. It is a fundamental requirement. If a guest arrives with a smile on his face and a twinkle in his bleary eye, it is a good sign: it is unlikely that he will die of boredom, and he might even get a small taste of bliss. Unlucky is the teetotaler who ventures into the Salon des Variétés. It is doubtful that he will take a shine to it, and when he gets home he will give his sons a good hiding so they will know better than to visit the salon when they grow up. Tipsy guests totter up the stairs, hand the doorman their ticket, enter the hall filled with portraits of the great, brace themselves, and plunge bravely into the hurly-burly, stumbling through all the rooms, from door to door, thirsting to catch a peek of something rare. They push and jostle as if looking for something. What a seething hodgepodge of faces, colors, and smells! Ladies—red, blue, green, black, variegated and piebald, like three-kopeck woodblock prints. The same ladies were here last year and the year before—and you will see them here next year, too. Not a single décolleté, as they are in corsets and bloomers and . . . have no busts worth mentioning. And what strange and marvelous names: Blanche, Mimi, Fanny, Emma, Isabella. You will not find a single Matryonna, Mavra, or Pelageya.

The dust is terrible! Specks of powder and paint hang in the air in a haze of alcoholic fumes. You cannot breathe, and the urge to sneeze tickles your nose.

"What a rude man you are!"

"Me? Ah . . . hmm, well, permit me to express to you in prose that I am fully up-to-date on feminine ideas. Allow me to escort you."

"How dare you, young man! You had better introduce yourself first, and wine and dine me a little!"

An officer hurries over, grabs the lady by the shoulders, turning her away from the young man so that she faces him. The young man is not pleased. He pauses, decides to take offense, grabs the lady by the shoulders, and turns her so she faces him again.

A big German with an oafish, inebriated face stumbles through the crowd. He emits a loud belch for all to hear. A pockmarked little man comes shuffling up behind him, clasps his hand, and shakes it.

"F-f-fool!" the German says.

"I wish to express my sincerest gratitude for your sincere belch," the little man says.

"Um . . . ja . . . th-th-thank!"

By the entrance a crowd has gathered. Two young merchants are gesticulating furiously at each other in blind hatred. One merchant is red as a lobster, the other pale. Needless to say, they are both drunk as lords.

"How about . . . I punch you in the mug!"

"You ass!"

"No, You're an ass yourself! You . . . philanthropist!"

"You rat! Why are you waving your arms around? Go on, punch me! Go on!"

"Gentlemen!" a woman's voice rings out from the crowd. "How unseemly to use such language in front of ladies!"

"And the ladies can go to hell too! I don't give a flying hoot for your ladies! I can feed and clothe a thousand of them! And . . . you, Katya, stay out of this! Why did he insult me when I didn't do anything to him?"

A dandy sporting a gigantic cravat hurries over to the pale merchant and takes him by the hand.

"Mitya! Your papa is here!"

"He c-c-can't be!"

"Upon my word, he is! He's sitting at a table with Sonya—he almost saw me, the old devil! We have to get out of here!"

Mitya glares at his opponent one last time, shakes his fist at him, and retreats.

"Tsvirintelkin! Come here! Raissa's looking for you!"

"I'm not interested in her, she looks like a weasel! I've found another one—Fräulein Luisa!"

"What? That tub of lard?"

"A tub of lard she might be, but she's a lot of woman, and a triple helping, too! Try getting your arms around *her*!"

Fräulein Luisa is sitting at a table. She is big, fat, sluggish as a snail, and covered in sweat. Before her on the table are a bottle of beer and Tsvirintelkin's hat. The outline of her corset bulges over the expanse of her gigantic back. She prudently hides her hands and legs; her hands are large, rough, and red. Only a year ago she was still living in Prussia, where she washed floors, made beer soup for the Herr pastor, and looked after the little Schmidts, Müllers, and Schultzes. Fate decided to disturb her peace: she fell in love with Fritz, and Fritz fell in love with her. But Fritz could not marry a poor woman. In his eyes he would have been a fool to marry a poor woman. Luisa vowed eternal love to Fritz, and left her beloved *Vaterland* for the cold steppes of Russia in order to earn herself a dowry. And so she goes to the Salon des Variétés

every night. During the day, she makes little boxes and cro-
chets tablecloths. Once she has got together the agreed-upon
amount of money, she will return to Prussia and marry Fritz.

"*Si vous n'avez rien à me dire . . .*" comes echoing from the
stage. There is a rumpus, applause for whoever happens to
be performing. A feeble cancan is underway: in the front
rows mouths are watering in delight. Look at the audience
as the women onstage shout "Down with men!" Give the
audience a lever, and it would turn the whole world upside
down. There is roaring, shouting, howling.

"Sss! Sss! Sss!" a little officer in the front row hisses at a girl.

The audience rises against the officer in furious indignation, and the whole of Bolshaya Dimitrovka Street rattles
with applause. The little officer gets up, and, his head high,
leaves the hall with a haughty flourish, his self-respect intact.

The Hungarian orchestra launches into a thunderous mel-
ody. What fat louts these Hungarians are, and how badly
they play! They are an embarrassment to their country.

The bar has been taken by storm. Behind the counter
is Monsieur Kuznetsov in person, standing next to a lady
with dark eyebrows. Monsieur Kuznetsov is pouring glasses
of wine, and the lady is collecting the money.

"A g-g-glass of vodka! You hear me? V-v-vodka!"

"Grab a glass, Kolya! Bottoms up!"

A man with short-cropped hair stares dully at his glass,
shrugs his shoulders, and avidly downs the vodka. "I
shouldn't, Ivan Ivanich, I have a heart condition."

"Nonsense! Nothing will happen to your heart condition
with a few drinks!"

The man with the heart condition downs another glass.

"Have another!"

"No, I've got a heart condition, and I've already had seven!"

"Nonsense!"

The young man downs another glass.

"Please, sir," a girl with a sharp chin and rabbit eyes whines, "buy me dinner!"

The man resists.

"I'm hungry. Just a little portion of something."

"What a nag you are! Waiter!"

The waiter brings a piece of meat. The girl eats. And how she eats! With her mouth, her eyes, her nose.

In a shooting booth bullets are whizzing. Two Tyrolean ladies are loading one rifle after another, and they are not at all bad-looking, either. An artist is standing next to them, drawing one of them on the cuff of his shirt.

"Thank you! Goodbye! Good luck to you!" the Tyrolean women shout as they leave.

As they leave the clock strikes two. The women onstage are still dancing. Noise, uproar, shouts, shrieks, whistling, a cancan. Oppressive heat and stuffiness. At the bar the drunks are getting drunker, and by three o'clock there is total mayhem.

In the meantime, in the private rooms . . .

Anyway, time to go! How wonderful it is to leave this place. If I were the owner of the Salon des Variétés, I would not charge customers at the entrance—but at the exit.

AN IDYLL—
BUT ALAS!

"My uncle is such a wonderful man," Grisha, Captain Nasechkin's hard-up nephew and sole heir, would say to me. "I love him with all my heart! Why don't you come meet him? It would make him so happy!"

Whenever Grisha spoke of his uncle his eyes filled with tears. And I will say to his credit that he was not ashamed of these tears and was quite prepared to cry in public. I accepted his invitation, and a week ago dropped by to see the old captain. When I entered the hall and peered into the drawing room, I witnessed a most touching scene. The wizened captain was sitting in a large armchair holding a cup of tea, and Grisha was kneeling next to him, tenderly stirring it. The pretty hand of Grisha's fiancée was caressing the old man's leathery neck, while she and Grisha squabbled as to who would be the first to shower the dear uncle with kisses.

"And now, sweet children of my heart, my sole heirs, you must kiss each other!" Captain Nasechkin spluttered with joy.

An enviable bond united the three. Even though I am a hard man, I must admit that my heart was gripped by joy as I gazed at them.

"Yes indeed!" Captain Nasechkin was saying to them. "I think I can say I've had a good life! And may God grant a good life to everyone! How many fine fillets of sturgeon I have enjoyed, like the one I ate back in Skopin! Even today it makes my mouth water!"

"Oh, tell us all about it!" I heard Grisha's fiancée plead.

"So there I was in the town of Skopin with all my thousands of rubles, and . . . er . . . I went straight to . . . er . . . Rikov . . . Yes, to Mr. Rikov. What a man! Good as gold! A gentleman! He received me like I was family . . . you'd have thought he wanted something from me . . . but no, like I was family! He served me coffee, and after the coffee, a little snack . . . and the table . . . the table was filled with bottles and food . . . and a big fat sturgeon . . . from one corner to the other . . . lobster . . . caviar. You'd have thought it was a restaurant!"

I entered into the drawing room; it happened to be the day on which news had just reached Moscow by wire that the Skopin Bank had collapsed.

After we were introduced, Nasechkin said to me: "I am rejoicing in the company of these sweet children!" And, turning back to them, continued proudly: "Not to mention, you only find the best society in Skopin . . . government officials, men of the cloth . . . priests, monks . . . with every glass of vodka, you get a blessing then and there . . . and the host was covered in so many medals that even a general would have gasped! The moment we finished the sturgeon they brought out another! We ate that one too. And then they brought out some fish soup . . . pheasants!"

"If I were in your shoes," I told the captain, "I would be having heartburn at today's news, but I must say I am amazed how well you are taking things. Did you lose a lot of money with Rikov?"

"What do you mean, 'lose'?"

"Lose money—when the bank collapsed!"

"Poppycock! Balderdash! Old wives' tales!"

"You mean you haven't heard the news? Good Lord, Captain Nasechkin! But that is . . . that is absolutely . . . Here, read this!"

I handed him the newspaper I had in my pocket. Nasechkin put on his spectacles and, smiling dismissively, began to read. The further he read, the paler and gaunter his face grew.

"It has co-co-collapsed!" he gasped, all his limbs begin-ning to quake. "Oh the calamities raining down on my poor head!"

Grisha's face flushed a deep purple. He read the article and turned white. His hand trembling, he fumbled for his hat. His fiancée tottered.

"My God!" I exclaimed. "Are you telling me that none of you knew? The whole of Moscow is agog!"

An hour later I was alone with the captain, still trying to comfort him.

"Don't worry, Captain Nasechkin! It isn't the end of the

world! You may have lost all your money, but you still have your darling nephew and his fiancée!"

"How right you are! Money brings trouble . . . but I still have those dear children . . . yes!"

But alas! A week later I ran into Grisha.

"Why don't you go see your poor uncle?" I asked him. "You really should—he hasn't seen hide nor hair of you!"

"He can go to hell for all I care!" Grisha said. "The old fool! Couldn't he have found himself a better bank?"

"Still, you ought to go see him! He's your uncle after all!"

"Him? You must be joking! What gave you that idea? He's my stepmother's third cousin thrice removed!

"Well, at least send your fiancée to see him."

"Yes, and as for that—I don't know why the devil you had to show her that newspaper before our wedding day! She's shown me the door. She was waiting to pounce on my uncle's goods and chattel too, the silly fool! You can imagine how disappointed she is!"

I realized that, without meaning to, I had destroyed a most idyllic trio.

A DOCTOR'S ROMANCE

On achieving physical maturity and bringing one's studies to completion, it is fitting to opt for *feminam unam* in addition to a dowry *quantum satis*.

That is precisely what I did: I took *feminam unam* (taking two wives is prohibited) as well as a dowry. Even the ancients called those to account who married without insisting on a dowry. (*Ichthyosaurus*, XII.3)

I prescribed for myself horses, a loge in the dress circle, began imbibing *vinum gallicum rubrum*, and bought myself a seven hundred–ruble fur coat. In short, I set out on a life of a *lege artis* nature.

My wife's *habitus* was passable. Height: average. Skin and mucous membranes: normal. Subcutaneous layer of fat: adequate. Chest: satisfactory (no crackling). Vesicular breathing: regular heart sounds.

Psychological diagnosis: the only deviation from the norm is that my wife is chatty and somewhat loud. I am now suffering from acoustic hyperesthesia of the right auditory nerve. Whenever I examine a patient's tongue I think of my wife, a thought that leads to an increased heart rate. How right the philosopher was who maintained: *Lingua est hostis hominum amicusque diaboli et feminarum.*

Mater feminae, my mother-in-law (a mammal), suffers from the same ailments as my wife: when the two of them spend twenty-three hours out of twenty-four shouting at the top of their lungs, I show signs of mental derangement, combined with suicidal tendencies.

As my esteemed medical colleagues will confirm, nine-tenths of all women suffer from a condition that Charcot has defined as hyperesthesia of the vocal organs. The remedy he suggests is amputation of the tongue, an operation with which he promises to rid mankind of one of its worst ailments. But alas! Billroth, who carried out this operation on numerous occasions, attests in his memoirs that after the operation women learned to speak by using their fingers, which had an even more deleterious effect on their husbands. (Memor. Acad., 1878) I propose a different course of treatment (cf. my dissertation). Amputation of the tongue should be performed, as Charcot proposes, but, relying on Professor Billroth's findings, I suggest combining said amputation with a directive that the subject be made to wear mittens. (I have noted that individuals suffering from muteness who wear mittens are wordless even when hung.)

AN EDITOR'S ROMANCE

A small, straight nose, a beautiful bust, delightful hair, and exquisite eyes—not a single typographical error. I line-edited her and we married.

"You must belong to me alone," I told her on the day of our wedding. "I will not tolerate your being serialized. Remember that."

The day after the wedding I already noticed a slight change in my wife. Her hair was not as lustrous, her cheeks not as beguilingly pale, her eyelashes not so diabolically black, but reddish. Her movements were not as soft, her words not as gentle. Alas! A wife is a bride that has been half disallowed by the censor.

In the first six months I surprised her with a cadet who was kissing her (cadets love complimentary pleasures). I gave her a first warning, and once more in the strictest possible terms forbade all general distribution.

In the second six months she presented me with a bonus: a little son. I looked at him, looked in the mirror, looked at him again, and said to my wife: "This is a clear case of plagiarism, my dear. It's as plain as the nose on this child's face. I will not be hoodwinked!" I added, issuing another warning, along with a ban that prohibited her from appearing before me for a period of three months.

But these measures did not work. By the second year of our marriage my wife had not one cadet, but a number of them. Seeing her unrepentant, and not wishing to share with colleagues, I issued a third warning and sent her, along with the little bonus, home to her parents so she could be under their watchful eye, where she is to this day.

Her parents receive monthly royalties for her upkeep.

THE TURNIP

A Folktale

Once upon a time a little old man and his wife lived happily, and a son was born to them whom they named Pierre. Pierre had long ears and instead of a head a fat turnip. He grew up to be a big, strapping fellow. The little old man tried pulling him up by the ears so something might come of him. He pulled and pulled, but to no avail. The little old man called his wife. The wife grabbed hold of the little old man and the little old man grabbed hold of the turnip, and they pulled and pulled, but still to no avail. The wife called in a princess, who happened to be her aunt.

The aunt grabbed hold of the wife, the wife grabbed hold of the little old man, the little old man grabbed hold of the turnip, and they pulled and pulled. But to no avail. The aunt called over a general, who happened to be her godfather.

The godfather grabbed hold of the aunt, the aunt grabbed

hold of the wife, the wife grabbed hold of the little old man, the little old man grabbed hold of the turnip, but still to no avail. The little old man was at his wit's end. He happened to have a daughter too, whom he gave to a rich merchant. He called in the merchant, who had many hundred-ruble bills to his name.

The merchant grabbed hold of the godfather, the godfather grabbed hold of the aunt, the aunt grabbed hold of the wife, the wife grabbed hold of the little old man, the little old man grabbed hold of the turnip, and they pulled and pulled, and finally managed to give the turnip all the pull it needed.

And the turnip became a great state councilor.

EASTER GREETINGS

An anteroom. A card table in the corner. On it are a government-issued sheet of gray paper, a pen, an inkpot, and some blotting paper. The usher is pacing up and down the hall, his mind on food and drink. On his well-fed countenance covetousness is written, and in his pockets the fruits of extortion jingle. At ten o'clock a little man—or an *individual*, as His Excellency likes to say—comes in from the street. The individual slips into the hall, tiptoes over to the table, picks up the pen timidly and with trembling hand, and begins writing his forgettable name on the gray sheet of paper. He writes slowly, with gravity and feeling, as if it were a calligraphic exercise. Lightly, very lightly, he dips the pen into the inkpot, four times, five—he is afraid the ink will spatter. A smudge and all will be lost! (There had been a smudge once, but that is a long story.) The individual does not end his signature with a flourish—he wouldn't dare. He draws the *r*'s in painstaking detail. He finishes his calligraphic daub and peers at it, checking for errors, and not finding any, wipes the sweat from his brow.

"A happy Easter to you!" he says to the usher, and the individual's dyed mustache brushes three times against the porter's prickly one as they exchange the ceremonial triple kiss. The sound of smacking lips is accompanied by the pleasant tinkle of the "small donation" dropped into the pocket of this modern-day Cerberus. This first individual is followed by a second, a third, a fourth, until one o'clock. The sheet of paper is covered with signatures from top to bottom. At four o'clock Cerberus disappears with the sheet into the inner chambers. He hands it to a little old man who begins reading it through.

"These are all the Easter greetings? Hmm . . . Ha! Hmm . . . Well, I don't recognize any of the handwriting! I tell you, one man is responsible for all these signatures! A calligrapher—they hired a calligrapher to write their Easter greetings! The audacity! I can see they didn't want to trouble themselves to come wish me a happy Easter in person! What have I done to deserve this? Why this lack of respect? (Pause.) Well . . . I say, Maksim, will you go and get . . ."

Eleven o'clock. A panting, sweating, flushed young man with a cockade on his military cap is clambering up the endless flights of stairs to the fifth floor. Having reached it, he frantically rings the bell. A young woman opens the door.

"Is Ivan Kapitonich at home?" the young man asks, still out of breath. "Tell him . . . tell him to hurry back to His

Excellency's! He must put his name down again on the list of Easter greetings! Someone stole the piece of paper! We need to put together a new list! Hurry!"

"Who in heaven's name would steal something like that?"

"That damned woman . . . that . . . that housekeeper of his! She gathers up all the paper she can find and sells it by the bale! The miserly old biddy, damn her! But I have eight more people to go tell—goodbye!"

Another waiting room. A table and a sheet of paper. An usher, ancient and thin as a rake, is sitting on a stool in the corner. At eleven o'clock the door from the inner chambers opens. A bald head peeks in.

"What? No one has come yet to wish me happy Easter, Efim?" a voice asks.

"No, Your Excellency."

At noon the same head peers in again.

"What? No one has come yet to wish me happy Easter, Efim?"

"Not a soul, Your Excellency!"

"Hmm . . . Ha! Hmm . . ."

The head peers in at one, at two—still nobody. At three o'clock a whole torso, complete with hands and legs, protrudes into the room. The little old man walks over to the table and stares intently at the empty sheet of paper. There is an expression of deep sadness on his face.

"Things aren't what they used to be, Efim!" he says with a sigh. "Hmm . . . hmm . . . well, the fatal word 'retired' is stamped on my forehead. The poet Nekrasov wrote something about that, didn't he? Efim, dear fellow, so my old woman doesn't laugh me out of house and home, let's fill up the sheet ourselves with an assortment of Easter greetings! Here's the pen . . ."

TWENTY-SIX

(Excerpts from a Diary)

June 2nd

After dinner, I pondered the sad state of the Western European economy. I hired her as housekeeper.

June 18th

She was quarrelsome during dinner. From what I can tell, she must be going through some kind of emotional upheaval. I fear she is having an affair. I read in one of the lead articles in *Golos* that . . . Madness!

December 4th

My gates were opening and shutting all night. At five in the morning I saw Karyavov the clerk leaving the courtyard. When I asked him what he was doing, he was embarrassed. He was obviously up to no good, the rascal. I will have to fire him.

December 28th
She has been quarrelsome all day long. I'm sure someone has been loitering about outside. I caught a mouse in file folder 1302. I killed it.

New Year's Day
Was wished a happy New Year. I presented her with an edifying book for her improvement. She was quarrelsome all day. Feeling despondent, I wrote a piece called "On the Pecheneg Raids in the District of Ufa." I had a vision.

January 4th
She tore up both the piece I wrote and the book I gave her. She ordered me to rehire Karyavov. Yes, my sweet darling, right away! That night she was quarrelsome, tore up my papers, flew into hysterics, and informed me that she was leaving for Samara for a rest cure. I will not let her go!

February 6th
She has left! All day I lay on her bed weeping, and have come to the following conclusion: "She is in the best of health and consequently cannot have gone for a cure." Something else is behind this—a love affair! I suspect that she might be drawn to one of my milksop clerks. But which one? I'll find out tomorrow, since the culprit is bound to ask for a leave, and I . . . I will give him a good hiding! The gates didn't keep opening and shutting last night, but I still slept badly. In spite of my dejection, I pondered the terrible state of France. I had two visions at the same time. Lord in heaven, forgive us sinners!

February 7th

I was handed twenty-six requests for leave. From all the clerks! Just you wait! They want to go to Kronstadt. Ha! So now Samara is in Kronstadt, is it? Just you wait!

February 8th

My grief has not diminished. I am deeply dejected. I have launched a reign of terror. All the clerks in the office are in a state of panic—the last thing on their minds is love. I dreamed of Kronstadt.

February 14th

Yesterday, Sunday, Karyavov went somewhere out of town, and today he is strutting about the office with a sarcastic smile on his lips. I am firing him.

February 25th

I received a letter from her. She is ordering me to send her money and to rehire Karyavov. "Yes, my sweet darling, right away!"

Just you wait, you rogues! Yesterday, three more clerks went somewhere out of town. Whose gates are they opening and shutting?

THE PHILADELPHIA CONFERENCE OF NATURAL SCIENTISTS

The first conference paper to be read was "The Descent of Man," dedicated to the memory of Darwin. Since the delegates in the large conference hall were linked to each other by telephone, the paper was read in a whisper. The distinguished reader stated that he was in full agreement with Darwin: the apes were at the bottom of it all. If there had been no apes there would have been no people, and had there been no people there would have been no criminals. The delegates agreed unanimously that all apes were to be advised of our displeasure, and that the public prosecutor was to be notified.

Some delegates did, however, voice certain doubts:

The French delegate was in full agreement with the other delegates' opinion, but at a loss to explain how one might account for the origins of, say, pigs in clover or crocodiles shedding tears. Having expounded on this point, the distinguished delegate presented diagrams of pigs in clover and teary-eyed crocodiles. The debate deadlocked, and it was proposed that the matter be postponed to the following session, and also that all telephones be disconnected before a final decision was reached.

The German delegate (who was also the foreign correspondent of the Russian Slavophile newspaper *Russ*), declared that he was leaning more toward the theory that man developed from a crossbreeding of apes and parrots. In his opinion, men were in the process of destroying themselves by their aping of foreign ways. (A buzz of approval was heard over the telephone lines.)

The Belgian delegate agreed with the other delegates to a certain extent, but in his opinion not all nations could have developed from apes. Russians, he argued, had evolved from thieving magpies, Jews from foxes, and Englishmen from frozen fish. He proved his theory about the Russians' magpie heritage quite convincingly, and as the other delegates were still under the sway of the big embezzlement trials going on in Moscow they were quite ready to adopt the Belgian delegate's thieving magpie theory. (*The Times*)

MY NANA

This was in the days before I became an unknown man of letters and before my bristling mustache had properly sprouted.

It was a beautiful spring evening. I was returning from a dacha soirée where we had danced as if possessed. In my whole youthful being there was—to put it figuratively—not a single stone left standing, not a phrase intact, not a single realm uncrushed. A desperate love raged in my frantic soul. It was a piercing, scalding, spirit-smothering love—my first love. I had fallen in love with a tall, well-built young lady of about twenty-three with a pretty but slightly foolish face and exquisite dimples on her cheeks. I fell in love with those dimples too, and with the light blond hair tumbling in curls over her beautiful shoulders from beneath her wide-brimmed straw hat.

Words escape me! Returning from the soirée, I threw myself on my bed and groaned as if I had been hit over

49

the head. An hour later I was sitting at my table, my whole body shivering, and wasted a good twenty sheets of paper trying to write the following letter.

My dearest Valeria Andreyevna,

I do not know you very well, indeed barely at all, but I will not let this hinder achieving my goal. Omitting grandiloquent turns of phrase, I shall come straight to the point: I love you! I love you more than life itself! This is not hyperbole. I am an honest man. I work (there followed a lengthy description of my virtues). My life is not dear to me. I am prepared to die—if not today, then tomorrow, and if not tomorrow, a year from now, what do I care! On the table before me, just two feet from my chest, lies a revolver (a six-shot .38 caliber). I am in your hands! If the life of a man who is passionately in love with you is in any way dear to you, then please respond to this letter. Your maid Palasha knows me. You can send a reply through her.

Sincerely,
The man who sat across from you yesterday

P.S. Have pity on me!

I sealed the letter and placed the revolver on the table in

front of me—more for effect than to take my life—then went outside and made my way past the dachas in search of a mailbox. A mailbox was found, and the letter dropped in.

And, as Palasha later told me, this is what happened to my letter. The next morning at about eleven, Palasha placed the letter, which the postman had just delivered, on a silver platter and took it up to her mistress' bedroom. Valeria Andreyevna lay beneath an airy silken cover, stretching lazily. She had just woken up and was smoking her first cigarette of the day. A ray of sunlight pierced the window, and she whimsically crinkled her nose. When she saw my letter, she made a sour grimace.

"Who's it from?" she asked. "Read it to me, Palasha. I don't like reading those letters. They're always so full of nonsense."

Palasha unsealed my letter and began reading it aloud. The more she read, the wider her mistress' eyes grew. When Palasha came to the part about the revolver, Valeria Andreyevna opened her mouth and looked at her in terror.

"What does he mean?" she asked in bewilderment.

Palasha repeated the words. Valeria Andreyevna's eyes blinked.

"Who is this man? Who is he? Why does he write such things?" she gasped. "Who is he?"

Palasha realized that I was the one who had written the letter, and described me.

"But why does he write such things? Why? What am I supposed to do? There's nothing I can do, is there, Palasha? Well . . . is he rich?"

Palasha, whom I had been tipping with almost everything

I earned, thought for a few moments, and then said it was quite likely that I was rich.

"But there's is nothing I can do, is there? I'm expecting Alexei Matveyich today, and the baron tomorrow . . . and on Thursday, Monsieur Romb. When am I supposed to receive him? It will have to be during the day, won't it?"

"You've arranged for Grigory Grigorevich to start visiting you during the day."

"You see what I mean! Can I receive him at all? Well, tell him . . . tell him . . . well, have him come to tea today. But that's the best I can do!"

Valeria Andreyevna was on the verge of tears. It was the first time in her life that she had been confronted with a revolver, and it had been through my pen! That evening I drank tea with her. Though I was suffering, I had four cups. As luck would have it, it began to rain, and Valeria's Alexei Matveyich did not visit her. In the end, I did rejoice.

FLYING ISLANDS

by Jules Verne
Translated by A. Chekhonte

CHAPTER I

The Talk

". . . And with this, gentlemen, I conclude my talk," said
Sir John Lund, a young member of the Royal Geographical
Society, and, exhausted, sank into his chair. The conference
hall resounded with applause and shouts of bravo, and one
after another the members came up to Sir John to shake
his hand. In token of their enthusiasm, seventeen gentlemen broke seventeen chairs and dislocated eight long necks
belonging to eight gentlemen, one of whom was the captain of the *Confusion*, a 100,009-ton yacht.

"Gentlemen," Lund began with some emotion. "I

consider it my duty to thank you for the infernal patience with which you sat through my talk, which lasted for forty hours, thirty-two minutes, and fourteen seconds"; and, turning to his old servant, he added, "I say, Snipe, wake me in five minutes; I'll be taking a nap, if these gentlemen will permit me forty winks in their presence."

"I shall wake you, sir," Old Snipe replied.

Lund leaned his head back and immediately fell asleep. He was a Scotsman by birth, who had had no schooling whatever, nor had he studied anything—but there was nothing he did not know. He belonged to that small number of happy natures that achieve knowledge of all that is great and wonderful through their intellect alone. The rapture his talk inspired was entirely merited. In the course of the forty hours, he had presented to the assembled gentlemen a grand project, which, if carried out, would bring much glory to Great Britain and demonstrate the heights to which the human intellect could soar. The topic of Lund's talk was "Drilling Through the Moon with a Giant Drill."

CHAPTER II

A Mysterious Stranger

Lund had not slept for three minutes when a heavy hand rested on his shoulder and he awoke. Before him towered a man two and a quarter yards tall, thin as a rake and drawn as a dried snake. He was quite bald, dressed entirely in black, and four pairs of spectacles were balanced on his nose. He was sporting two thermometers, one on his chest and one on his back.

"Would you be so kind as to follow me?" the bald-headed gentleman said in a sepulchral voice.

"Whither?"

"Follow me, Sir John."

"And if I do not?"

"Then I might be constrained to drill through the moon before you do."

"In that case, sir, I am at your service."

"Your manservant may accompany us."

Lund, the bald-headed man, and Tom Snipe left the lecture hall, and the three of them made their way through the gaslit streets of London. They walked quite a distance.

"If you please, sir," Tom Snipe said to Lund, "if our way is to be as long as this gentleman is tall, then the laws of friction dictate that we will wear down the soles of our shoes to nothing."

The two gentlemen gave Tom Snipe's words ten minutes' thought, and, finding them not without wit, laughed out loud.

"With whom, may I ask, do I have the honor of sharing a good laugh?" Lund asked the bald-headed gentleman.

"You have the honor of walking, laughing, and conversing with a member of every geographical, archaeological, and ethnographical society in the world, doctor of all past and present fields of science, member of the Moscow Arts Circle, honorary trustee of the Southampton School of Bovine Obstetrics, subscriber to *The Illustrated Devil*, professor of greenish-yellow wizardry and introductory gastronomy at the future University of New Zealand, and director of the Anonymous Observatory, William Dunderheadus. I, sir, am taking you to . . ."—John Lund and Tom Snipe bent their knees in reverence before the great man of whom they had heard so much, and bowed respectfully—"I am taking you, sir, to my observatory, which is located twenty miles from here. I, sir, need a partner for an enterprise, the meaning of which you will only be able to grasp using both hemispheres of your brain. My choice fell upon you. But after a forty-hour talk, I doubt that you will be in a condition to enter any kind of conversation, and I, sir, love nothing more than my telescope and lasting silence. Your manservant's tongue, I hope, will follow your command. Long live speechlessness! I am taking you to . . . I hope you don't mind."

"Not in the least, sir. My only regret is that we are not fast walkers and have no soles on our shoes, since they cost money, and—"

"I shall buy you new shoes."

"Thank you, sir."

Readers who wish to familiarize themselves further with Dr. Dunderheadus can turn to his remarkable study, "Did the Moon Exist Before the Great Flood, and if so, why did it not ink?" Along with this study was also published a banned pamphlet written a year before his death: "How to Crush the Universe to Powder Without Perishing." These works characterize, like no other, this most remarkable of men. Among other things he describes how he lived for whole time in the Australian swamps, where he survived on crabs, mud, and crocodile eggs, and in the two years did not once see fire. While there, he invented a microscope just like the ones we have, and discovered the bones of a fish belonging to the Pisces family. Returning from his long journey, he settled some miles outside London and dedicated himself entirely to astronomy. Being a convinced misogynist (he had been married three times, as a consequence of which he sported three pairs of formidable horns), and not wanting to be the butt of every joke, he withdrew to live the life of an ascetic. As he possessed a fine, diplomatic intellect, he was clever enough to make certain that his observatory and astronomical findings were known to him alone. Regrettably, and to the misfortune of all true-blooded Englishmen, this great man did not live on into our times. He quietly passed away last year, swallowed by three crocodiles while swimming in the Nile.

CHAPTER III

Mysterious Spots

In the observatory to which Dr. Dunderheadus took Lund and Old Tom Snipe—(there follows an excruciatingly long and boring description of the observatory, which the translator has refrained from rendering with a view to saving space and time)—stood the telescope the doctor had perfected. Lund walked over to it, and began to look at the moon.

"And what do you see, sir?"

"The moon, sir."

"But what do you see next to the moon?"

"I have the honor of seeing the moon and nothing but."

"But can't you see the moving white spots next to the moon?"

"By Jove, sir! Call me an ass if I do not see the spots you speak of! What manner of spots are they?"

"They are spots only visible through my telescope. Enough, leave the telescope. Sir John, I wish to find out, nay, must find out what those spots are! I will be there soon enough! I shall travel to them, and you must accompany me!"

"Hurrah! Long live the spots!" Sir John and Old Snipe called out in unison.

CHAPTER IV

A Rumpus in the Skies

A half hour later Dr. Dunderheadus, Sir John Lund, and Tom Snipe were already flying toward the mysterious spots in eighteen balloons. They were sitting in a hermetically sealed cube filled with condensed air and chemicals for the production of oxygen.* This grandiose flight, the likes

---

* A smell invented by chemists. They say one cannot live without it. Fiddlesticks. It is only without money that man cannot live. (A. Chekhonte, the translator)

of which no man ever ventured on, was undertaken on the thirteenth of March, 1870. A southwesterly wind was blowing. The magnetic needle was pointing NWW. (There follows an extremely boring description of the cube and the eighteen balloons.) A deep silence reigned in the cube. The two gentlemen sat wrapped in their coats, smoking cigars, while Tom Snipe lay stretched out on the floor, sleeping as if he were at home in his bed. The thermometer* indicated that the temperature was below the freezing-point. During the first twenty hours not a word was spoken, and nothing particular happened. The balloons entered the cloud zone, a number of lightning bolts chasing but not reaching them as they were British. On the third day, John Lund fell ill with diphtheria while Tom Snipe suffered an attack of bile. The cube collided with an asteroid and received a dreadful thump. The thermometer indicated a temperature of minus seventy-six degrees centigrade.

"How are you keeping, sir?" Dr. Dunderheadus finally asked Lund on the fifth day, breaking the silence.

"Thank you for your concern," Lund replied, touched by the doctor's solicitude. "I am suffering most profusely. Where is my trusted manservant?"

"He is sitting in a corner chewing tobacco, and attempting to look like a man married to ten women at the same time."

"Ha ha, I say, that's a good one, Dr. Dunderheadus!"

"Thank you, sir."

The doctor was about to shake Lund's hand when

---

* Such an instrument does in fact exist. (A. Chekhonte, the translator)

something terrible happened. There was a great rattling and a shattering bang, the thunder of a thousand cannons, a frenzied, howling piping noise. The brass cube, having fallen into a layer of thin space, could not bear the inner pressure and exploded, its shreds hurtling into endless distances.

It was a terrible moment, the most singular in history!

Dr. Dunderheadus grabbed hold of Tom Snipe's legs, who in turn grabbed hold of John Lund's legs, and the three of them, with lightning speed, plummeted into endless depths. One after the other the balloons tore away, and, freed from all weight, spun in circles, exploding with deafening bangs.

"Where are we, sir?" John Lund inquired of the doctor.

"In the ethers."

"I say, if we are in the ethers, what are we to breathe?"

"Where, Sir John, is your strength of will?"

"Gentlemen," Tom Snipe called out, "I have the honor of informing you that for some reason we are not falling downward, but upward!"

"I see . . . Damn it all! That means we are no longer within the earth's gravitational pull . . . That means our goal is drawing us toward it! Hurrah! Sir John, how is your health holding up?"

"Thank you for your concern. But, sir, I see the earth above us."

"That isn't the earth—it is one of our spots. We will crash into it any moment now."

Bang!

CHAPTER V

Prince Meshchersky Island

The first to regain consciousness was Tom Snipe. He rubbed his eyes and let them wander over the terrain on which he, Dr. Dunderheadus, and John Lund were lying. He took off one of his stockings, and with it began rubbing the gentlemen down, who immediately regained consciousness.

"Where are we?" John Lund asked.

"We are on an island that belongs to a group of flying islands!" the doctor replied. "Hurrah!"

"Hurrah! Look up there, doctor!" Lund called out. "We have outshone Columbus!"

Above them a number of other islands were floating (a description follows that would only make sense to Englishmen). The three men set out to reconnoiter the island. Its measurements were (Verne gives us numbers and more numbers—to hell with them!). Tom Snipe managed to find a tree whose sap was redolent of Russian vodka. Strangely enough, the trees were no taller than grass. (Balderdash!) The island was uninhabited. No living creature had ever set foot on it before.

"I say, doctor, what might this be?" Lund said to Dr. Dunderheadus, picking up some sort of package.

"Strange . . . most extraordinary . . . what a surprise!" the doctor mumbled.

Inside the package were the writings of a certain Prince Meshchersky, composed in some barbarian language, probably Russian.

"How could these writings have ended up here?"

"A thousand damnations!" Dr. Dunderheadus shouted. "Have others beaten us to these islands? Who could it be? Tell me, who, who? Damn them! O thunderbolts of heaven, dash my—rather large—brain to smithereens! If I get my hands on him, if only I could get my hands on him! I'll tear him to pieces, along with his works!" And raising his hands in the air he laughed a terrible laugh. A disquieting glint flickered in his eye. He had gone mad.

CHAPTER VI

The Return

"Hurrah!" the inhabitants of Le Havre called out, crowding onto all the quays of the town. The air was filled with shouts of joy, tolling bells, and music. The massive black object in the sky that had threatened everyone with death was about to fall not onto the town but into the harbor. All the ships were hurrying out into the open sea. The massive object that had covered the sun for so many days splashed heavily into the bay, inundating the waterfront, to the accompaniment of thundering music and the triumphant hullabaloo of the people. It began to sink, and within a few minutes the bay was free again, waves surging through it in every direction. In the middle of the bay three men were floundering. These were mad Dr. Dunderheadus, John Lund, and Tom Snipe, who were quickly pulled out of the water by a nearby boat.

"We haven't eaten in fifty-seven days," muttered John Lund, who was as thin as a starving artist, as he told the people what had happened.

The island of Prince Meshchersky no longer exists. Bearing the weight of three intrepid men, it grew heavier, and leaving its orbit fell into the earth's gravity and plummeted into the harbor of Le Havre.

Conclusion

These days, John Lund is once again occupying himself with the question of drilling through the moon. The day is nigh when the moon will be graced with a hole, a hole that will belong to Great Britain. Tom Snipe is currently living in Ireland, where he has dedicated himself to farming. He raises chickens and apportions good hidings to his only daughter, whom he is bringing up in spartan fashion. He is not a stranger to scientific matters, and is quite angry at himself for having neglected, while on the flying island, to gather seeds of the tree whose sap is redolent of Russian vodka.

A BRIEF ANATOMY OF MAN

On an examination a student was asked: "What is man?" He replied: "An animal." After some thought, he added: "But . . . a rational one." The enlightened examiners agreed only with the second part of his answer; on the first part, the student was given an F.

Anatomically speaking, a man consists of:

A skeleton, or "skellington" as some of our military medics and provincial teachers call it. The skeleton smacks of death. Covered in a sheet, it will frighten you to death; without one, it will frighten you too, but not to death.

A head. Everyone has one, but not everybody needs one. Some believe that heads were given us so we can think, others so we can wear hats. (The second belief is less dangerous.) Sometimes heads contain brain matter. A police supervisor, present at the autopsy of a man who had suddenly dropped dead, on seeing the brain asked the doctor what it was. "That is what people think with," the doctor replied. The police supervisor grinned contemptuously.

A face. The mirror of the soul (except in the case of lawyers). It has many synonyms: physiognomy, countenance (*facies*, or *continentia* as the priesthood might say), visage, mug, ugly puss, etc.

A forehead. Its functions: to touch the floor as one kneels begging for favors, and to bang against the wall when said favors are not accorded. (Consequently, the forehead often reacts to gold.)

The eyes. These are the police commissioners of the head. They see all and make a note of everything. The blind man is like a town abandoned by the authorities. In days of sorrow, eyes weep. But during the happy times in which we live, they only weep with emotion.

The nose. We have been given noses for nasal colds and our sense of smell. It is best not to stick noses into politics. Sniffing has been known to increase the revenues generated by the tobacco tax, which is why the nose can be counted among man's useful organs. At times a nose is red, but not because it is freethinking (at least, that is what the experts claim).

The tongue. According to Cicero it is the *hostis hominum et amicus diaboli feminarumque.** As denunciations are nowadays written on paper, tongues have been sent packing. In women and snakes, tongues serve to pass the time. The best kind of tongue: boiled.

The nape. Is only of use to the Russian peasantry, for the yoke to rest on.

The ears. Ears are drawn to cracks in doors, open windows, tall grass, and flimsy fences.

---

* An enemy of man and a friend of the devil and women. [Translator]

The hands. They write satirical pieces, play the violin, seize, apprehend, lead away, confine, beat. For the simple man, hands provide a living; for those not so simple, they serve as a means to distinguish right from left.

The heart. A repository for patriotic and many other sentiments. In women the heart is like an inn: the ventricles are occupied by the military, the atria by civilians, the apex cordis by the husband. The heart looks like the ace of hearts in a deck of cards.

The waist. The Achilles' heel of ladies who read fashion magazines, nude models, seamstresses, and warrant officers with lofty ideals. A favorite among young bridegrooms and corset sellers. The second target when a young man declares his love. (The first target is a kiss.)

The paunch. This is not a body part one is born with, but a part one acquires. It grows according to the rank of the councilor. A state councilor without a paunch cannot sit in state. (By Jove, the perfect pun!) Ranks below that of the court councilor do not have paunches, but bellies; merchants have guts, and merchants' wives wombs.

The groin. Has not been sufficiently studied by science. According to house porters it is located somewhere above the knee, while according to field medics it is found somewhere below the chest.

The legs. These grow out of the place nature invented to be struck by the rod. Legs are extensively used by postmen, debtors, reporters, and messengers.

The heels. Where one finds the souls of guilty husbands, men whose tongues have just slipped, and soldiers fleeing the field of battle.

A CHILDREN'S PRIMER

INTRODUCTION

Dear little ones,

Only the just and the honest can be truly happy in this world. Bastards and scoundrels can never be happy, and therefore you have to be honest and just. You must not cheat at cards—not because you might get bashed over the head with a candlestick, but because it is dishonest. You must honor your elders—not because you will be given a good hiding, but because it is what fairness demands. For your edification, I have gathered some stories and tales.

Miserliness Does Not Pay

Once upon a time three friends—Ivanov, Petrov, and Smirnov—went to a tavern to have lunch. Ivanov and Petrov were not misers, and ordered a sixty-kopeck lunch. Smirnov, on the other hand, being a miser, refused to order any food. They asked him why.

"I don't like the cabbage soup they serve in these taverns," he told them. "And furthermore, all I have left is sixty kopecks. A man has to keep some money for cigarettes. I think I'll just have an apple!"

Smirnov ordered an apple and began eating it, looking enviously at his friends eating cabbage soup and tasty dishes of poultry. But the thought that he had managed to save some money comforted him. One can imagine his astonishment when the bill came: Two full meals—one ruble and twenty kopecks. One apple—seventy-five kopecks. From that day on he ceased being a miser, and never again bought fruit at taverns.

Taunt Not Thy Neighbor

A five-ruble coin struck up a conversation with a one-ruble plate of food, and began to taunt it.

"My friend!" he said to the one-ruble plate of food. "Take a look at me! I am a lot smaller than you, but worth quite a bit more, not to mention the shine I give off! Though my actual value is set at five rubles and fifteen kopecks, people are already paying a good eight rubles for me!"

The coin continued taunting the one-ruble plate of food

for quite a long time. The plate of food listened and listened, but said nothing. A little later the plate of food came across a one-ruble banknote and said to it: "I feel so sorry for you, you poor piece of paper, you! How ridiculous you look! Though my actual value is set at one ruble, people are already paying a ruble and a quarter for me in taverns, while you are now worth even less than your official value! Shame on you!"

"My dear friend," the one-ruble banknote replied, "you and your friend the five-ruble coin have reached your grandeur on account of my fall. But nevertheless I'm glad to have been of some service to you."

The one-ruble plate of food blushed with shame.

Blatant Ingratitude

Once upon a time a pious man gathered together in his courtyard on his name day all the lame, blind, crippled, and purulent of the town and gave them food. He offered them watery cabbage soup, peas, and raisin pies.

"Eat and rejoice in the Lord, my brothers and sisters!" he told the beggars. They ate without a hint of gratitude. After the meal, the crippled, lame, blind, and purulent said a hasty prayer and left.

"Well? How was the pious man's food?" a constable standing near the pious man's gate said to one of the lame beggars.

The lame man waved dismissively and limped on. The constable asked one of the purulent beggars the same question.

"All he did was spoil our appetite!" the purulent beggar replied indignantly. "They're burying Yarlikov the merchant today, and we're all going to his funeral feast."

A Fitting Retribution

There once was a naughty boy who was in the habit of scribbling indecent words on walls. He scribbled them convinced he would not be punished. But, dear children, all bad deeds are punished. One day the naughty boy walked along a wall, took out a piece of chalk, and wrote for all to see: "Fool! Fool! Fool!" People walked past and read it. A clever man walked by, read the words, and went on his way. A fool walked by, read the words, and took the naughty boy to court for defamation.

"I am not taking him to court because his words have insulted me," the fool maintained, "but out of principle!"

Excessive Diligence

There once was a newspaper plagued with maggots. The editor in chief called in the marsh birds and told them: "Gobble up all those maggots!" The birds began pecking away, and pecked up not only all the maggots but the whole editorial office, along with the editor in chief.

Truth Will Out

As he lay dying, King Darius of Persia called his son Ataxerxes to his side. "My son, I am dying," he said to him.

"After my death you must call together all the wise men of the world and have them solve the riddle I will tell you. Appoint the men who solve the riddle as your ministers."

Leaning forward, Darius whispered the riddle into his son's ear.

After his father's death, Ataxerxes called together all the wise men of the world.

"Wise men!" he proclaimed. "My father ordered me to ask you the following riddle. Whoever solves it will become my minister.

Ataxeres told them the riddle. The wise men were five in number.

"But who will check our answers, Your Majesty?" one of the wise men asked the young king.

"No one will," Ataxerxes answered. "I trust your word. If you assure me that you have solved the riddle, I will believe you without putting you to the test."

The wise men sat around a table, and began trying to work out the riddle. That very day, toward evening, one of the wise men appeared before Ataxerxes and said: "I have solved the riddle."

"Excellent. I herewith appoint you as my minister."

The following day three more wise men solved the riddle. Only one wise man, Artazostra, remained seated at the table. He could not solve the riddle. A week passed, a month passed, and Artazostra still sat at the table struggling to solve the riddle. A year passed. Two years passed. Pale, thin, and haggard, he sat there filling hundreds of sheets of paper with scribbles, and yet he was nowhere near finding the solution.

"Put him to death, Your Majesty!" the other wise men who had solved the riddle said to the king. "He has tricked you by passing himself off as a wise man!"

Yet Ataxerxes did not put Artazostra to death, but waited patiently. Five years later, Artazostra appeared before the king, fell to his knees, and said: "Your Majesty! This riddle is unsolvable!"

The king helped the wise man to his feet, kissed him, and said: "You are right, wise man! This riddle is in fact unsolvable. With your words you have answered the one question that weighed heavily on my heart: You have proved to me that there are still honest men in the world. And as for you," he said, turning to his four ministers, "you are nothing but swindlers!"

Perturbed, one of the four ministers asked: "I suppose you want us to leave?"

"No! Stay!" Ataxerxes said to them. "Swindlers though you are, I need you."

And thank God, they did stay.

For Evil Too Let Us Be Thankful

"O almighty Zeus! Powerful hurler of thunderbolts!" a poet once prayed to Zeus. "Send me a muse to inspire me!"

Ancient history was not one of Zeus's strong points. So it should come as no surprise that he made a mistake, and instead of sending Melpomene he sent Terpsichore to the poet. Terpsichore appeared before the poet, and the poet, instead of composing ditties that he could sell to magazines, went and enrolled in dance classes. He danced for a hundred days and a hundred nights, and then suddenly thought: "Zeus did not listen to me. He is making fun of me. I prayed for inspiration and he has taught me how to do a jig!"

And the poet impudently wrote a scathing ditty about Zeus. The Olympian god hurled down a thunderbolt at him. The poet died.

Conclusion

And so my dear children, do good and you shall triumph.

SOOTHSAYER AND SOOTHSAYERESS

Nanny is reading the old quartermaster's fortune.

"I see a road."

"Where to?

Nanny waves her hand northward. The quartermaster's face turns white.

"You will be traveling with a money sack on your knees," the old woman adds.

Bliss floods the quartermaster's face.

A civil servant is sitting with two lit candles, looking into the mirror. He wants to divine the height, complexion, and temperament of his new superior, whom he has not yet met. He gazes into the mirror for an hour, two, three.

Tremors flit over his eyes, little sticks fly past, feathers flutter about—but no superior of any kind. He sees nothing: no superiors, no inferiors. A fourth hour passes, a fifth . . . He has had enough of waiting for the new superior. He stands up, waves his hand dismissively, and sighs.

"I see the position will remain unfilled," he says. "That is not good at all. Anarchy will reign!"

A young lady is standing by the gate in her yard waiting for someone to walk by. She has decided that the first passer-by's name will be that of her future betrothed.

Someone is approaching.

She quickly opens the gate and calls out, "May I ask your name, sir?"

The answer to her question is a loud moo, and through the half-open gate she sees a large dark head. Upon this head is a pair of horns.

"So that's what his name will be," the young lady thinks to herself. "I hope his face will be different, though."

The editor of a daily newspaper is trying to read the fortune of his offspring in some coffee grounds.

"Give it up," his deputy editor tells him. "This is pointless. Give it up, I tell you!"

The editor is not listening, and continues to stare into the coffee grounds.

"I see many images," he says. "The devil knows what they are. I see some gloves! Ah, a hedgehog! And here's a nose . . . it's the spitting image of my son Makar's nose! And here's a baby calf . . . I have no idea what any of this means.

The doctor's wife is looking into the future with the help of a mirror and sees . . . coffins.

"That can only mean somebody will die," she thinks. "Or . . . that my husband's practice will flourish this year."

THE
VAUDEVILLIAN

Ivan Akimovich Sparrov-Falkonov, a vaude-villian, thrust his hands into the pockets of his wide trousers, turned to face the window, and fixed his languid eyes on the house across the street. Five minutes of silence ensued.

"How tiresome!" Maria Andreyevna, an ingénue, said with a yawn. "Why don't you say something, Ivan Akimovich? You drop in to see me and keep me from learning my lines, so at least *say* something! How intolerable you are, I must—"

"Well . . . umm . . . there is something I would like to ask you, but . . . how shall I put it? If I just blurt it out, like some lout, well, you would laugh at me . . . No, I will not speak! I will hold my tongue!"

"I wonder what he wants to ask me?" the ingénue thought. "How agitated he is, and that strange glint in his eye, and how he keeps shuffling from one foot to the other . . . He's not going to declare his love, is he? Oh, what fools men are! Yesterday the first violin proposed, today the raisonneur spent the whole rehearsal sighing—boredom has driven them all insane!"

The vaudevillian left the window and walked over to the dressing table, where he eyed the nail clippers and jars of rouge. "Well . . . um . . . you see, I want to ask you something, but I am afraid . . . I feel so awkward. If I blurt it out just like that you will say: 'The boor! The peasant!' I know you so well, Maria Andreyevna! No, I will hold my tongue!"

"But what should I say to him if he really does declare his love?" the ingénue pondered. "He's a good enough man, well-known, talented, but, well, I really don't like him. He isn't much to look at, his shoulders droop—and what about those warts on his face? His voice is shrill, and those mannerisms! No! Never!"

The vaudevillian began pacing up and down the room in silence. He slumped heavily into an armchair, and noisily snatched up a newspaper lying on the table. His eyes darted over the pages as if they were looking for something. They stopped on one of the smudged letters and sagged.

"If only there were some flies buzzing around!" he grumbled. "That would at least brighten things up a little."

"If you think about it, his eyes aren't that bad," the ingénue mused. "But the best thing about him, I suppose, is his character. After all, the soul and mind of a man are far more important than his looks. Well . . . I could see myself married to him, but living with him without a ring is absolutely out of the question! How he looked at me just now!

Obviously his senses are inflamed! But why is he so timid?
I simply don't understand!"

The vaudevillian sighed deeply and smacked his lips. His
silence was clearly weighing heavily on him. He turned red
as a lobster. His mouth twisted to the side. There was a look
of anguish on his face.

"Well, do I really need a ring?" the ingénue mused. "He does
earn a good salary, and living with him would be better than
living with some roughneck of a sea captain. Fine! I will tell him
that I'm prepared to live with him! Why hurt the poor man's
feelings by turning him down? His life is hard enough as it is."

"No! I must speak!" the vaudevillian spluttered, rising
from the armchair and throwing the newspaper aside. "I
can't control my damned nature! I can't hold back! Beat me,
curse me if you will, Maria Andreyevna, but I must speak!"

"Speak! Speak, for heaven's sake!"

"Maria Andreyevna, my dear, sweet Maria Andreyevna! I
beg you . . . I beseech you, I implore you on bended knee . . ."

The vaudevillian's eyes filled with tears.

"For goodness' sake! Speak!"

"Tell me, my sweet Maria Andreyevna, could I . . . could
I possibly have a glass of vodka, just a tiny little glass? My
soul is on fire! After yesterday's drinking bout my mouth
is so oxidized, transoxidized, superoxidized, that no chem-
ist in the world can deoxidize it! I appeal to you from the
depths of my soul! I'm at the end of my tether!"

The ingénue blushed, frowned, but quickly composed
herself, and brought the vaudevillian a glass of vodka. He
emptied it, livened up, and began telling her a string of
playful anecdotes.

DIRTY TRAGEDIANS AND LEPROUS PLAYWRIGHTS

A Dreadful, Terrible, and Scandalously
Foolhardy Tragedy
A play of many Acts, and even more Scenes

Dramatis Personae

MIKHAIL VASILEVICH LENTOVSKY: a man, and a theater impresario.

TARNOVSKY: a playwright who is on nodding terms with devils, whales, and crocodiles; has a pulse of 225, and a temperature of 109.4.

CHARLES XII: King of Sweden; struts like a fireman.

THE BARONESS: a brunette not without talent; willing to take on lesser roles.

GENERAL EHRENSVÄRD: a hulking fellow of a man with the voice of a mastodon.

JAKOB DE LA GARDIE: an unremarkable man; delivers his lines with the panache of a . . . prompter.

STELLA: Lentovsky the impresario's sister.

BURL: a man carried on the shoulders of dim-witted Svobodin.

THE GRAND MAÎTRE DU BALLET HANSEN.

AND OTHERS.

*Epilogue**

Scene: The crater of a volcano. A blood-drenched desk at which Tarnovsky is sitting; in lieu of a head on his shoulders, there is a skull. Sulfur is burning in his mouth, and from his nostrils sniggering little devils hop. He dips his pen—not into an inkpot, but into a cauldron of lava stirred by witches: a terrifying spectacle. Ants of the kind that scurry down one's back fly through the air. Downstage, quivering sinews hang on glowing hooks. Thunder and lightning. We see the calendar of Aleksey Suvorin (the province and district secretary), which foretells with the passionless detachment of a bailiff the collision of the earth with the sun, the destruction of the universe, and the rise in prices for all pharmaceutical commodities. Chaos, terror, fear . . . I leave the rest to the reader's imagination.

---

* I wanted to leave "Prologue," but the editor insists that the less believable all this is, the better. Fine by me.

TARNOVSKY (*chewing his pen*)

What should I write, dammit? I can't think of anything! *A Journey to the Moon?*—No, that's been done already . . . *The Hunchback?*—That's been done too. (*He takes a sip of burning oil.*) I must come up with something . . . something that will make the wives of Moscow merchants dream of devils for three nights in a row. (*He massages his forehead.*) *Avanti*, O great brain! (*He ponders; thunder and lightning; the salvos of a thousand cannons as represented in one of Fyodor Shechtel's illustrations. Dragons, vampires, and snakes slither out of cracks. A large box falls into the crater, out of which Lentovsky emerges, holding a big poster.*)

LENTOVSKY

Hey there, Tarnovsky!

TARNOVSKY, THE WITCHES, AND ALL THE OTHERS
(*together*)

Greetings, Your Excellency.

LENTOVSKY

Well, dammit? (*He brandishes a club at him.*) Is the play ready?

TARNOVSKY

No, it isn't, Mikhail Valentinich. I sit here thinking, but can't come up with anything. The task you have set me is too difficult! You want the blood in the audience's veins to freeze, you want earthquakes to grip the hearts of the wives of Moscow merchants, you want all the lamps to be doused by my monologues. But you must see that this is beyond the powers of even a great playwright like me, Tarnovsky!

Having praised himself, Tarnovsky becomes flustered.

LENTOVSKY

Balderdash, dammit! A good dose of gunpowder, a Bengal sparkler, and grandiose monologues—that's all you need! To satisfy the wardrobe department, dammit, set the play in high society. Treason . . . Prison . . . the prisoner's beloved will be forced to marry the villain . . . We can give the role of the villain to Pisarev. Then an escape from prison . . . shots . . . no need to scrimp on the gunpowder . . . a young maiden whose noble origins come to light only during the course of the play . . . Finally more shots, a conflagration, and the triumph of virtue . . . In short, a play baked in the mold of *The Adventures of Rocambole* or *The Count of Monte Cristo* . . .

Thunder, lightning, hoarfrost, dew. The volcano erupts; Lentovsky rushes out.

Act I

The audience, ushers, the Grand Maître du Ballet Hansen, and others.

USHERS
(taking the audience members' furs)

A small tip, Your Excellency? (*Not receiving one, they grab the public by the coattails.*) Oh black thanklessness! (*They are ashamed for humanity.*)

A MEMBER OF THE AUDIENCE
So, is Lentovsky over his illness?

ORCHESTRA CONDUCTOR
He's been kicking up a fuss, so he must be better.

THE GRAND MAÎTRE DU BALLET HANSEN
(*changing in the dressing room*)
I'll knock 'em dead! I'll show them! All the newspapers will sing my praises!

The First Act continues, but the reader is no doubt impatient: he's waiting for the Second Act. So, curtain.

Act II

The Palace of Charles XII. Backstage, our grand set designer Valtz is swallowing swords and red-hot coals. Thunder and lightning. Enter Charles XII and his courtiers.

CHARLES XII
(*pacing the stage and rolling his eyes*)
De la Gardie! You have betrayed the fatherland! Hand over your sword to the captain and off to prison with you!

De la Gardie utters a few heartfelt words and exits.

CHARLES XII

Tarnovsky! In your harrowing play you have made me live an extra ten years! Off to prison with you! (*To the Baroness*) You love De la Gardie and have a child by him. In the interest of the plot, however, it would be better if I knew nothing about that and give you in marriage to a man you do not love. Marry General Ehrensvärd!

BARONESS
(*marries the General*)
Ach!

General Ehrensvärd is appointed warden of the jail in which De la Gardie and Tarnovsky are being held.

GENERAL EHRENSVÄRD
I'll make their life hell!

CHARLES XII
Well, that's it for me until Act V. I'm off to the dressing room!

Acts IV and V

STELLA
(*who usually is not such a bad actress*)
Count, I love you!

YOUNG COUNT
And I love you too, Stella. But, in the name of love, I beseech you, tell me why Tarnovsky had to put me in this

damn play. It goes on forever! What does he need me for? What in God's name does this plot have to do with me?

> BURL

It's the octopus that's behind all this. It was only because of the octopus that I ended up a soldier. He beat me, hounded me, bit me . . . He is the one who wrote this play, or my name isn't Burl! He'll do anything to make my life hell!

> STELLA
> (*realizing her noble origins*)

I shall go to my father and free him!

On the way to the prison she meets the Grand Maître du Ballet Hansen. He executes a few entrechats.

> BURL

It's all because of the octopus that I ended up a soldier and am now in this play, and it's the octopus that has made Hansen dance in order to make my life hell! Well, we'll see about that!

Bridges fall. The scene is engulfed. Hansen executes a great leap that makes the elderly spinsters in the audience faint.

> *Acts V and VI*

In the prison Stella meets her father for the first time and they come up with a plan to escape.

STELLA

I shall save you, Father . . . But how can we flee without Tarnovsky joining us? If he should escape prison, he will write a new play!

GENERAL EHRENSVÄRD
(*torturing the Baroness and the prisoners*)
As I am a villain, I must not resemble a human being! (*He eats raw meat.*)

De la Gardie and Stella escape from the prison.

ALL

Stop them! Catch them!

DE LA GARDIE

Whatever happens, we shall escape and achieve our goals! (*A shot is fired.*) Damn! (*He drops dead.*) And damn that too. For just as the author can assassinate, he can just as well resuscitate!

Charles XII appears from the dressing room and commands virtue to triumph over evil. There is universal jubilation. The moon smiles, and so do the stars.

THE AUDIENCE
(*calling out to Burl, pointing at Tarnovsky*)
There's the octopus! Catch him!

Burl strangles Tarnovsky, who falls to the ground dead but immediately jumps up again. Thunder, lightning, hoarfrost, the dénouement of the play Two Mothers, *or* He Was Run Over by a Locomotive, *mass migration, shipwreck, and the gathering of all the pieces.*

LENTOVSKY

I'm still not satisfied. (*He is engulfed with the rest of the scenery.*)

MARIA IVANOVNA

A young woman of about twenty-three was sitting in a luxuriously furnished drawing room on a purple velvet sofa. Her name was Maria Ivanovna Odnoschekina.

"What a trite, stereotypical beginning!" the reader gasps. "These writers always begin their stories in luxuriously furnished drawing rooms! I don't want to read this!"

I beg my reader for forgiveness, and continue. A young man of about twenty-six, with a pale, somewhat sad face, stood before her.

"Here we go again! I knew it!" the reader snaps. "A young man, and twenty-six of all things! So what comes next? I know! He spouts poetry, declares his love, and she tells him in an offhand manner that she wants him to buy her a bracelet! Or the opposite, she wants poetry, but he . . . oh, I can't bear this!"

Be that as it may, I shall continue. The young man's eyes were fixed on the young woman as he whispered: "I love you, you marvelous creature, even though the chill of the grave envelops you!"

Here the reader loses all patience and begins to curse. "Damn you all! You writers serve up the most idiotic piffle with luxuriously furnished drawing rooms and Maria Ivanovnas enveloped by the damn chill of graves!"

Who knows, dear reader, perhaps you are right to be angry. But then again, perhaps you are not. We live in great times precisely because it is impossible to tell who is in the right and who in the wrong. Even a jury convicting a man for committing theft does not know where the guilt lies: In the man? In the money that just happened to be lying around? In the jurors themselves for having been born? You can't tell what's what in this world!

Anyway, even if you are right it doesn't mean that I am wrong. You think my story is not interesting, that it is pointless. So let's assume that you are right and I am wrong. But I beg you at least to take extenuating circumstances into consideration. Can I be expected to write something interesting and important if I am despondent and if I have been suffering from intermittent bouts of fever?

"So don't write if you have a fever!"

Fine. But let me get straight to the point—let's say I have a fever and am in a bad mood, and that another author has a fever, and a third a jittery wife and a toothache, and a fourth is suffering from depression. None of us would be writing! And where do you think the newspapers and magazines would get their material? Perhaps from the tons and tons of little stories and anecdotes that you, the readers, keep sending in day after day? From the tons of piffle you send in and from which we would be lucky, lucky indeed, to extract just one salvageable piece.

We are all professional literati, not dilettantes! We are literary day laborers, each and every one of us is a person, a person just like you, like your brother, like your sister-in-law—we have the same nerves, the same innards, we are tormented by the same cares that torment you, and our sorrow is much greater than our joy will ever be, and if we wanted to we could come up with reasons not to work every day! Each and every day! But if we were to listen to your "Stop writing!"—if we were all to give in to our fatigue, or despondency, or fever, then we might as well close down all of modern literature!

But we must not close down all of modern literature, dear reader, not for a single day. Even if to you it looks pointless and dull, uninteresting, even if it inspires no laughter or anger or joy in you, literature still exists and serves a purpose. We need literature. If we walk off and leave our calling behind, even for a minute, fools in dunce caps with bells on them will replace us, bad professors, bad lawyers, and bad cadets marching in lockstep, describing their absurd amorous escapades.

I *have* to write, regardless of how despondent I might be or whether or not I have intermittent bouts of fever! I have to, in any and every way I can, without stopping! There are so few of us—you can count us on the fingers of one hand—and when there are so few workers in a business, you cannot ask for a leave, even a short one—not that you would be given one.

"But still, you writers could choose topics that are a little more serious! I mean, what is the point of this Maria Ivanovna? Is there such a lack of incidents to write about? Is there such a lack of important issues?"

You are right, there are many incidents to write about and many important issues to discuss, but why don't you tell me exactly what you would like me to write? If you are so indignant, why don't you prove to me once and for all that you are right, that you really are a serious person living a serious life. Go on, prove it to me in concrete terms, or I might be led to think that the incidents and issues you are talking about don't amount to much, and that you are simply one of those nice enough fellows one meets who, having nothing better to do, likes to chitchat about *serious matters*. But I must finish the story I started:

The young man stood awhile before the beautiful woman. Finally he took off his frock coat and shoes, and whispered, "Farewell till tomorrow!" Then he lay down on the couch and drew a plush coverlet over himself.

"In the presence of a lady!" the reader shouts indignantly. "This is pure rubbish! It's an outrage! Police! Censor!"

Wait a moment, wait a moment, my stern reader. The lady in the luxuriously furnished drawing room was painted in oils on a canvas that is hanging above the couch. So feel free to be as outraged as you like.

"But how can your magazine put up with this? If they are printing rubbish like 'Maria Ivanovna,' then it's obviously because they don't have anything better. That's a plain and simple fact. Sit down immediately, expound your deepest and most exquisite thoughts, cover a good ream of paper

with your writing, and send it off to an editorial. Sit down
and write! Write everything down and send it out!"

And soon enough it will be sent right back.

TROUBLING
THOUGHTS

A classics instructor of severe, inflexible, bilious aspect but a secret dreamer and freethinker, complained to me that whenever he oversaw student presentations or attended teachers' meetings, he was tortured by troubling and unsolvable questions. Invariably, he complained, his mind was assailed by matters such as: What would happen if the floor were the ceiling, and the ceiling the floor? Are ancient languages profitable or unprofitable? How would instructors be called before the director if his office were located on the moon? These and similar questions, if they persistently preoccupy one's mind, are referred to by psychiatrists as "obsessive thoughts." It is a troubling, incurable ailment, but fascinating for the onlooker. The other day, the instructor approached me and said he was preoccupied by the issue of what would happen if men dressed like women. An incongruous, even uncouth question perhaps, though not one particularly difficult to answer. The classics instructor himself provided the following response. If men dressed like women, then:

Low-ranking members of the civil service, such as collegiate registrars, would appear in calico dresses, though on high feast days perhaps in muslin ones. They would wear one-ruble corsets and striped stockings made of paper. Décolletés would only be permitted when they were among themselves;

Postmen and reporters who raise their skirts to step over ditches and puddles would be called to account for outraging public decency;

Moscow's great littérateur, Sergey Andreyevich Yuriev, would walk about in crinolines and a cotton bonnet;

School guards Mikhei and Makar would appear before the director every morning to lace him into his corset;

Officers on special assignments and secretaries of charitable societies would dress beyond their means;

Maikov the poet would wear his hair in ringlets, and appear in a green dress with red ribbons and a cap;

The ample frame of the Pan-Slavist leader Ivan Aksakov would be draped in the flowered smock of a village babushka;

The directors of the Lozovo-Sevastopol Railways would, on account of their poverty, strut about in petticoats.

And as for the conversations:

"Your bodice is above all criticism, Your Excellency, and the bustle is excellent. Your décolleté might, however, be a little low."

"Nonsense, old boy, my décolleté follows the guidelines set by our table of ranks. It's a Grade 4 décolleté. By the way, can you straighten my ruffle?"

LETTER TO A REPORTER

Sir:

I know everything! There were six big fires this week and four tiny ones. A young man shot himself in a conflagration of passion for a young lady, whose head, upon hearing of his death, went astray. Guskin, a house porter, hanged himself after excessive imbibification. A boat drowned yesterday, along with two passengers and a small child . . . poor child! At the Arkadia, someone burned a hole in the back of a merchant's jacket, and in the ensuing rumpus he nearly had his neck broken. Four swindlers dressed to the nines were apprehended, and a train capsized. I know everything, my dear sir! As many exciting things have happened this week as you have rubles in your pocket, of which you haven't given me a single kopeck of what you owe me!

A gentleman does not act this way!

Your tailor,
Smirnov

RUSSIAN COAL

A True Story

Count Tulupov was traveling down the Rhine on a boat one fine April morning and, having nothing better to do, struck up a conversation with a *Kraut*. The German—young and angular, bristling with haughty scholarliness and staunch self-esteem in his starched collar—introduced himself as Arthur Imbs, a mining specialist, and launched into an extensive discourse on Russian coal, a topic that, try as he might, the bored count could not divert him from.

"Indeed, the fate of our coal is most lamentable," the count interrupted with the sigh of the knowledgeable expert. "Lamentable! St. Petersburg and Moscow are running on British coal, Russia is burning her virgin forests in its ovens, and all the while there are vast reserves of coal lying buried in the south!"

Imbs shook his head wistfully and, clicking his tongue in indignation, asked to see a map of Russia.

The count's manservant brought a map and the count ran his finger along the shores of the Sea of Azov and then over Kharkov: "There . . . around here . . . you see? The whole south!"

Imbs wanted more precise information about the exact location of the coal fields, but could not induce the count to be more specific. The count's finger darted randomly over the length and breadth of Russia, and, wanting to stress the coal riches of the Don region, skidded as far south as Stavropol. The Russian count, it seemed, was not overly familiar with his country's geography. He was quite startled, even incredulous, when Imbs informed him that the Carpathian Mountains belonged to Russia.

"I have an estate in the Don region, you know," the count said. "Some twenty thousand acres of land, a superb estate! As for coal, it has . . . *eine zahllose . . . eine ozeanische Menge*! Millions of tons are buried there, just going to waste! It's always been my dream to do something about this. I've been waiting to come across the right man to help me—but we have no specialists in Russia! Not one!"

They began to talk about specialists. They talked and talked. Suddenly the count jumped up as if stung by a bee, clapping his hand to his forehead. "What a stroke of luck that we ran into each other!" he shouted. "What would you say if I asked you to come to my estate? Why stay here in Germany? Germany is teeming with learned Germans, while if you come to my estate you'll be able to do some good, some real good! How about it? Say you will!"

Imbs paced the cabin with a grave expression, weighing the offer. He agreed to come to Russia. The count clasped his hand, shook it enthusiastically, and called for champagne.

"Finally, after all these years, my mind is at peace!" the count told him. "Now I will have coal!"

A week later Imbs set out for Russia laden with books, charts, hopes, and impure thoughts of Russian rubles. In Moscow the count gave him two hundred rubles and the address of his estate, and told him to head south. "Why not go there now on your own and start work. I might perhaps come down in the autumn. Write and let me know how things are going."

Imbs arrived at Tulupov's estate, settled down in one of the mansion's wings, and the following day set about preparing to supply the whole of Russia with coal.

Three weeks later he sent the count a letter.

"I have familiarized myself with the coal on your land," he wrote, after a timid and protracted beginning, "and have come to the conclusion that due to its low quality it is not worth digging up. And even if it were three grades higher in quality, it would still not be worth touching. Not to mention that there appears to be a complete lack of demand for coal. Your neighbor, the coal magnate Alpatov, has fifteen million *poods* of coal ready for shipment, but cannot find a single buyer willing to give him even a brass kopeck for a *pood*. Not one sack of coal has ever traveled over the Donetsk coal line that passes through your estate, even though the tracks were specifically laid for that purpose. I would be dishonest or reckless if I gave you the slightest hope of success. I would also respectfully venture to add that your estate is in such total disrepair that thinking of coal prospecting or any other enterprise could be considered quite futile."

At the end of his letter the German asked the count if he could recommend him to another Russian nobleman—*"Fürsten oder Grafen"*—or send him *"ein wenig"* money for his return to Germany.

While Imbs waited for a reply, he busied himself with fishing for carp and trapping quail by whistling on a little pipe.

When the reply arrived, it was addressed not to Imbs but to Dzerzhinski, the Polish steward of the estate.

"And tell that German he doesn't know what the hell he's doing!" the count added in a postscript. "I showed his letter to an engineer (Privy Councilor Mleyev) and he split his sides laughing! You can tell the German that I'm not holding him back! He's free to go whenever he wants! I gave him two hundred rubles—if he spent fifty rubles to get there, he still has a hundred and fifty left!"

When the Pole informed Imbs of the count's letter, Imbs panicked. He sat down and filled two sheets with overwrought Germanic handwriting. He begged the count to magnanimously forgive him for having refrained from touching on "a few important details" in his first letter. With tears in his eyes and tormented by pangs of conscience, he wrote that in a card game with Dzerzhinski he had imprudently lost the 172 rubles that had remained after his trip from Moscow. "But afterwards I won back 250 rubles, and yet Dzerzhinski refuses to give them to me, even though I had paid him readily enough when he won. That is why I permit myself the indelicacy of throwing myself on Your

Grace's mercy, and beg you to compel the highly esteemed Mr. Dzerzhinski to pay me at least half the sum he owes me, so that I may leave Russia and no longer eat your bread for naught."

Much water flowed under the bridge and many carp and quail were caught by Imbs before the count replied. Toward the end of July the Pole came into Imbs' room, sat down on his bed, and began rattling off every curse he knew in the German language.

"What a royal ass the count is!" he said. "He writes that he is about to leave for Italy, but doesn't give any instructions about you! What am I supposed to do with you? Chop you up and eat you for dinner? And I don't know what got into him with that damned coal! He needs it as much as I need to have you hovering around here all day! And you're a fine one too! A blithering fool talks big to you out of sheer boredom and you fall for it!"

"The count is leaving for Italy?" Imbs asked, turning pale. "But did he send me any money? No? How am I supposed to leave if I don't have a kopeck to my name? I beg you, my dear Mr. Dzerzhinski, if you cannot give me the money I won from you, at least let me sell you my books and charts. Here in Russia you can get a lot of money for them!"

"Who needs your books and charts in Russia?"

Imbs sat down and thought. While the Pole filled the air with his curses, the German tried to figure out how to save his hide, and with all his German feelings felt his blood turning sour. His body shrank and sagged, and his air of haughty scholarliness yielded to hopelessness and pain. The realization of inescapable captivity far from the gentle waves of the Rhine and the convivial company of other mining engineers reduced him to tears. At night he sat by the window, gazing at the moon. There was silence all around. Somewhere in the distance a harmonica moaned a plaintive Russian song. The sound tore at his heart; he was overcome by such a powerful longing for his homeland and for fairness and justice, that he would have given his life to find himself back in Germany that very night.

"The same moon shines there as it does here—but what a difference!" he thought.

All night Imbs lay steeped in melancholy. Toward morning he could stand it no longer and decided to leave. He packed the books and charts that nobody in Russia needed into his knapsack, filled his empty stomach with water, and at precisely four in the morning left the estate and began walking north. He decided to head for Kharkov, over which the count's pink finger had darted not too long ago. Imbs was hoping to find Germans there who would lend him money for the journey home.

"And would you believe it, they even stole the boots off my feet as I lay sleeping by the roadside!" Imbs told a friend a month later as he sat on the deck of the same boat traveling down the Rhine. "So much for Russian honesty! But one thing I will say for Russian honesty: I slipped the train conductor forty kopecks I had gotten for my pipe, and he looked the other way and let me ride without a ticket all the way from Slavianska to Kharkov! Perhaps no honesty there, but what a bargain!"

THE ECLIPSE

Memorandum No. 1032

There is to be an eclipse of the planet moon on September the twenty-second at ten o'clock at night. This phenomenon, far from being unlawful, is in fact of some possible educational benefit (if seen from the point of view that even planets must frequently subject themselves to the laws of nature), I propose that Your Excellencies order that on said evening all street lanterns in your districts shall be lit so that the darkness of night will not prevent officials and townsfolk from seeing the eclipse. I also urge Your Excellencies to ensure that every precaution be taken to hinder any gathering of crowds in the streets, shouts of joy, and other such behavior that said eclipse might occasion. I ask you to inform me of all persons who might interpret this natural phenomenon subversively, should there be such persons (which I doubt, as I know how sensible townsfolk generally are).

Gnilodushin
Witnessed by: Secretary Tryasunov

———

Re: Memorandum No. 1032

In response to document no. 1032 circulated by Your Excellency, I have the honor to inform you that in my district we have no street lanterns, for which reason the eclipse of the planet moon took place in full darkness of the air, which, however, did not prevent many of the people assembled from perceiving said eclipse with fitting clarity. No infringement of the general peace and quiet or subversive interpretations or expressions of dissatisfaction were ascertained, except for one instance when the son of Deacon Amfiloch Babelmandebsky, a tutor, in response to a question from one of the townsfolk as to the cause of said eclipse of the planet moon, launched into a lengthy explanation clearly subversive for

healthy minds. I did, however, not understand the gist of his explanation, as he
spoke in scientific terms using many foreign expressions.

Ukusy-Kalanchevsky

———

Re: Memorandum No. 1032

In answer to Your highly esteemed
Excellency in matters of document no.
1032, I have the honor to inform you that
in the province entrusted to my care there
was no eclipse of the moon, though some
phenomenon of nature did in fact manifest
itself in the sky, which led to a darkening
of the lunar light, though I cannot say
with certainty whether this was the eclipse
or not. Following an exhaustive search,
three street lanterns were ascertained to be
in my district, which, after scrubbing the
glass and the insides, were lit. But these
measures did not have the desired results,
for said eclipse took place at a moment
when the lanterns, as the result of a gust of
wind blowing through their broken glass,
went out, and hence could not illuminate
the eclipse referred to in Your Excellency's

memorandum. There were no gatherings, as all the townsfolk were asleep except for one clerk of the district council, Ivan Avelev, who was sitting on the fence and peering at the eclipse through his fist, grinning equivocally. "Same to me whether there's a moon or not . . . I don't give a hoot!" he said. When I informed him that these words were whimsical, he boldly declared: "What are you defending the moon for, lamebrain! You'll be sending it season's greetings next!" And he added an immoral expression in local parlance, which I will have the honor of reporting him for.

Glotalov
Witnessed by: A man without a spleen

A PROBLEM

I would like to present the following problem for the reader to solve:

At two o'clock in the morning my wife, my mother-in-law, and I left the house where we had been celebrating the marriage of a distant cousin. At the feast, needless to say, we had eaten and drunk our fill.

"In my condition I can't go on foot," my wife announced, turning to me. "Kirill, darling, can you get us a cab?"

"A cab? What will you think of next, Dasha!" my mother-in-law protested. "With the price of everything these days, and us having to scrimp and save for every loaf of bread! We don't have a stick of wood for the stove, and you want a cab? Ignore her, Kirill!"

But valuing my wife's health and the fruit of our unhappy love (the reader will already have guessed that my wife was expecting), and finding myself at that stage of blissful tipsiness when walking provides an excellent impetus for understanding Copernicus' theory of the earth's rotation, I ignored my mother-in-law's entreaties and called to a cabbie. The cab pulled up . . . and this is the problem:

We all know the measurements of an average cab. I am a man of letters, from which it follows that I am thin and underfed. My wife, too, is thin, though somewhat broader than I am, since the will of fate has widened her diameter. My mother-in-law's diameter, on the other hand, is immense, her length equaling her width, her weight close to four hundred pounds.

"We won't all fit in a single cab," I said. "We'll have to take two."

"Are you stark raving mad?" my mother-in-law gasped. "We have no money to pay the rent, and you want to hire two cabs? I won't allow this! I withhold my blessing! A curse on this scheme!"

"But dearest mamasha," I said to my mother-in-law in as reverential a tone as I could muster, "you must see that the three of us simply cannot squeeze into this cab. Once you take a seat, by God's bounty, the cab will be full. Thin as I am, I might possibly be able to squeeze in next to you, but owing to her delicate condition our Dasha simply won't be able to squeeze in beside you. Where would she sit?"

"Do as you please!" my mother-in-law snapped, waving her hand dismissively. "The Lord has clearly sent you to torment me. But I withhold my blessing in the matter of a second cab!"

"Well, let me see . . ." I began, thinking aloud. "Thin as I am, I could sit with you, though then there would be no place for Dasha . . . and if I sit with Dasha, there'll be no place for you . . . Wait a minute! If, say, I sat with you, Dasha could sit on our knees. Although now that I think of it, that's physically impossible, since these cabs are so damned narrow. Well, if, say, I sit with you, Mother, and you, Dasha, sit up on the box next to the cabbie . . . Dasha, how about sitting next to the cabbie?"

"Next to the cabbie?" my mother-in-law gasped. "I am a widow of high social standing! I will not allow a daughter of mine to seat herself next to some provincial lout! Has anyone ever heard the like? A lady sitting up on the box next to a cabbie!"

"In that case, how about this," my resourceful wife ventured. "Mother will sit in the back, as is proper, and I'll sit on the floor at her feet. I can huddle up and steady myself on the empty spot next to Mother, while you, Kirill, can sit with the cabbie . . . Your family has no standing worth mentioning, so there's no harm in your sitting up on the box."

"Yes, that might work. And yet," I said, scratching my head, "as I admit to being slightly tipsy, what happens if I fall off the box?"

"Slightly tipsy? Ha!" my mother-in-law countered. "Well, if you're so afraid of falling off, why not stand on the footboard and hold on to the back of the cab. We'll go slowly—you won't fall off."

Inebriated though I was, I could only spurn this shameful suggestion. A Russian man of letters clinging willy-nilly to the back of a cab! That would be the end of civilization as we know it! Exhausted from all the drinking and the perplexing puzzle I was facing, I was ready to throw up my hands and go home on foot when the cabbie leaned down to us and said:

"How about trying this . . ."

He offered us a solution to the problem that we all accepted.

What was this solution?

P.S. As an aid to the less nimble-minded among my readers, the cabbie's solution had me sitting next to my mother-in-law, while my wife was close enough to be able to whisper in my ear, "Kirill, you're jabbing me with your elbow. Move back a little!" The cabbie was sitting in his place. Surely the reader can now guess our configuration.

The solution:

I sat next to my mother-in-law with my back to the cabbie, my legs dangling out the back of the cab. My wife stood in the cab in the space where my legs would have been if I had been sitting like a normal human being, and steadied herself by holding on to my shoulders.

ON THE CHARACTERISTICS OF NATIONS

(From the Notebook of a Naïve Member of the
Russian Geographic Society)

The French are noted for their frivolity. They read immoral novels, marry without their parents' consent, do not obey doormen, do not respect their elders, and fail to read *The Moscow News*. They are so devoid of morals that their courts are overwhelmed with divorce cases. Sarah Bernhardt, for instance, divorces husbands with such regularity that through her patronage one court secretary alone grew richer by two houses. French women act in operettas and stroll along Nevsky Prospekt, while the men bake French bread and sing the Marseillaise. Many of their names rhyme with gigolo: Monsieur Rigolo, Monsieur Tremolo, Monsieur Ex-Nihilo, to name a few.

The Swedes waged war against Peter the Great and

gave our compatriot Lapshin the idea of Swedish matches (though they have not yet taught him how to make them work). Swedes ride Swedish horses, listen to Swedish ladies sing in restaurants, and grease the wheels of their carts with Norwegian tar. They live in remote areas.

The Greeks are mainly involved in trade. They sell sponges, goldfish, wine from Santorini, and Greek soap. Greeks who lack trading permits lead monkeys on leashes, or teach ancient languages. In their free time they fish near the Odessa and Taganrog customs offices. The Greek feeds on the bad-quality food served in Greek taverns, which is what ultimately leads to his demise. From time to time one comes upon a tall Greek such as Mr. Vlados, who runs a Tatar restaurant in Moscow—a man who is very tall and very fat.

Spaniards strum their guitars night and day, fight duels outside windows, and exchange letters with Constantine Shilovsky, a country squire from Zvenigorod, who composed "Baby Tiger" and "Oh to Be a Spaniard." They are never accepted into the civil service, as they have long hair and wear plaids. They marry for love, but kill their wives soon after the wedding in a fit of jealousy, despite the protestations of the Spanish police officers, who are highly respected in Spain. They engage in the preparation of Spanish fly.

Circassians, to a man, sport the title "Your Excellency," drink Georgian wine, and brawl in editorial offices. They are engaged in the production of antique Caucasian weaponry. Their minds are entirely unclouded by thought, and their noses are long so they can be led out by them of public places, where they cause disorder.

Persians battle Russian bedbugs, fleas, and cockroaches, for which they concoct Persian powder. They have been waging this war for a long time but it is far from won, and judging by the girth of merchants' feather beds that are stuffed with banknotes, and the cracks in the bureaucrats' beds through which banknotes slip away, victory is not in sight. Wealthy Persians sit on Persian carpets, poor Persians sit on stakes, a position the former find far more pleasurable. They wear the Imperial Order of the Lion and Sun, which is held by our very own Julius Schreyer, cannoneer and war correspondent extraordinaire, who garnered Persian sympathies. Another recipient of this order is the bankrupt director of the Skopin Bank, who received it for untiring services rendered to Persia, as many Moscow merchants also did for their unfaltering support of the Persians' aforementioned war on insects.

The British put an exceedingly high value on time. "Time is money" is their motto, and therefore, instead of paying their tailors what they owe them, they pay them from time to time. The British are busy: they give public speeches, sail about in boats, and poison Chinese with opium. Leisure is a foreign concept to them. They have no time for dinner, no time to spend at balls, no time for tête-à-têtes, no time for steam baths. They send menservants to their rendezvous, who are given carte blanche. (Children born to these menservants are recognized as legitimate.) This busy nation lives in British clubs and on the Promenade des Anglais. The Englishman feeds on Epsom salts, and succumbs to the English disease.

A MODERN GUIDE TO LETTER WRITING

What is a letter? It is one of the means by which thoughts and feelings are exchanged; and yet, as letters are so often written by people lacking all thought and feeling, this definition does not quite hit the mark. The best definition, perhaps, was once provided by a lofty postal clerk: "A letter is a noun without which postal clerks would end up jobless and stamps unsold."

There are open letters and sealed letters. The latter have to be opened with the utmost care, and, after having been read through, resealed carefully so that the addressee's suspicions are not aroused. Reading other people's mail is generally not to be recommended—although, of course,

123

the benefit those close to the addressee might gain from doing so warrants the practice. Parents, wives, and superiors interested in a person's morals, thoughts, and the purity of his convictions must read his letters.

Letters should be written with clarity and discernment. Courtesy, respect, and modesty of expression serve to ornament every letter, and when writing a letter to one's superiors in the civil service, these considerations, as well as carefully following the scale of rank in addressing one's superiors, is a prerequisite. You might, for instance, begin your letter in the following fashion: "Most magnanimous and beneficent Excellency, Ivan Ivanovich, May I draw your illustrious attention to . . ."

Men of letters, artists, and painters have neither rank nor title, so a simple "Dear Mr." will do.

SAMPLE LETTERS

A letter to one's superior

Most magnanimous and beneficent Excellency!

I am taking it upon myself to draw your exalted attention to the fact that yesterday, at the Chertobolotovs' christening, our assistant bookkeeper Peresekin repeatedly delivered himself of, among other things, the opinion that the floors of our chambers need to be relacquered, and that it was high time our tables had new coverings. Though I cannot imagine that there was any malicious intent in his statements, one can only discern in them a certain discontent with the current state of affairs. It is to be lamented that among us there are still some whose frivolity leads them to be blind to the benefits of our association with Your Excellency. What ends are these people pursuing? I am puzzled and aggrieved! Exalted Excellency! You shower myriad benefactions upon us, but, Your Excellency, deliver us from those who are heading toward an evil end and dragging others with them.

Yours in abject sincerity and prayerful devotion,
Semyon Gnusnov

P.S. With all respectfulness, I draw Your Excellency's attention to the fact that Your Excellency condescended to promise my nephew Kapiton the post of assistant bookkeeper. Though he might not yet have attained the highest standards of accomplishment, he is deferential and a teetotaler.

A letter to one's inferior

The day before yesterday, when you brought my galoshes over to my wife, you stood waiting in a draft and, I am told, caught a chill, leading to your absence from the office. You are herewith severely reprimanded for this gross negligence of your health.

A love letter

Dearest Mariya Ermeyevna,

Being in dire need of funds, I herewith offer you my heart and hand. To avert any doubts you might have, I am enclosing an affidavit from the police testifying to my character.

With tender love,
M. Tprunov

A letter to a friend

My dearest friend Vasya,

Could you lend me five rubles until tomorrow?

Yours,
Hypochondriakov

(Such a letter is to be answered with: "No, I can't.)

A business letter

Chère Princesse Milictrisse Kirbitevna,

May I, in abject respectfulness, draw Your Excellency's attention to Your Excellency's debt of one ruble and twelve kopecks that I had the honor of winning from Your Excellency in a game of cards the year before last at Beloyedov's house, but have not yet had the honor of receiving.

In humble expectation, etc.
Zelenopupov

A risky letter

Excellency!

Yesterday I learned quite by chance that the New Year's bonus I received was not owing to my personal merit, but to my wife's. Needless to say, under these circumstances I can no longer continue my service in your office, and must request a transfer.

With assurances of my utmost contempt, etc.

Yours, So-and-so

A letter of invective

Dear Sir!

You critic, you!

A letter to a writer

Dear Sir,

Though I do not know you personally, charity and pity for you drive me to proffer you some good advice (since you seem to be a capable enough person): give up your pointless attempts!

A well-wisher

(It is best to refrain from signing such a letter, as one might find oneself compromised.)

MAN AND DOG CONVERSE

It was a frosty moonlit night. Alexei Ivanovich Romansov brushed what he took to be a little green devil off his sleeve, carefully opened the gate, and entered the courtyard.

"Man is nothing but a mirage," he philosophized, "man is but ashes and dust. Pavel Nikolayevich might well be the governor, but he too is nothing but ashes and dust. His grandeur is just a hazy dream—one puff and he's gone!"

"Grrrr!" the philosopher heard.

He turned in the direction of the growl and saw a large black wolf-like dog, of the kind bred by the shepherds of the steppes. The dog was by the gatekeeper's hut, pulling at its chain. Romansov looked at the animal in astonishment, and thought awhile. He shrugged his shoulders, shook his head, and smiled dejectedly.

"Grrrr!" the dog repeated.

"No! I don't understand any of it!" Romansov proclaimed, throwing his arms up in the air. "And you . . . you have the gall to growl at a man? That's unheard of! Damnation upon you! Aren't you aware that man is the crown of creation? Look at me! I will now walk up to you. See? Am I a man, yes or no? What do you think? Am I a man or am I not a man? Out with it!"

"Grrrr! Woof!"

"Your paw!" Romansov said, reaching out his hand. "Your paw! You refuse? You prefer to withhold your paw? Very well. I will make a note of that. In the meantime, allow me to pat you . . . just an affectionate little pat—"

"Woof! Woof! Grrrr! Woof!"

"Ah, so you want to bite me, do you? All right! I'll remember that! So you don't give a hoot that man is the crown of creation, the king of animals! And I take it you would even be prepared to bite the governor himself! Am I right? The whole world prostrates itself before him, but you don't care who he is, or how important he is! Do I understand you? Aha! I see! So you are a Socialist! Stay where you are! I demand an answer!"

"Grrrr! Woof! Woof!"

"Stay where you are! Don't bite me! Now where was I? Oh yes—ashes and dust. One puff and he's gone! Puff! And why are we even alive, you ask. Our mothers give birth to us in agony, we eat, drink, learn the lessons of life, die . . . and what for? Dust! Man is worthless. You are just a dog and don't understand a thing, but if you . . . if you could peer into man's soul! If you could fathom man's psychology!"

Romansov turned away and spat.

"Nothing but dirt! You think that I, Romansov, collegiate assessor, am the king of nature! Well, let me inform you that you are wrong! I am a parasite, a crook, a hypocrite! The lowest of the low!"

Romansov banged his fist against his chest and began to weep.

"A damn sneak, a damned informer! Are you under the impression that Yegor Kornyushkin wasn't fired because of me? And if you don't mind my asking, who pilfered the committee's two hundred rubles and then blamed Surguchov? Are you going to tell me it wasn't me? I'm the lowest of the low! A Pharisee! A Judas! A toady! A usurer! A swine!"

Romansov wiped away his tears with his sleeve and began to sob loudly.

"Bite me! Tear me to pieces! From the day I was born no one has ever said an honest word to me . . . Everyone thinks I'm a low-down scoundrel, but to my face they only smile and praise me! If only someone would beat me or curse me out! Go on, bite me! Go on! Tear me to pieces, scoundrel that I am, a damned traitor!"

Romansov tottered and fell down on top of the dog.

"That's it, bite me! Chew my face to bits! Go ahead! Even if it hurts, show no mercy! There, my arms too! Yes, I see blood flowing! Serves you right, you scoundrel! Yes! *Merci beaucoup*, Zhuchka . . . that's your name, isn't it? *Merci!* And tear my coat to pieces, too! Who cares, the coat was a bribe too. I sold out another man and used the money to buy this coat! And the cap with the cockade! But what am I babbling on about? It's high time I got going. Goodbye, you sweet little doggie, you . . . you naughty little girl!"

"Grrrr!"

Romansov patted the dog, let it bite his calf one last time, wrapped his coat tightly about him, swayed, and tottered toward his door.

When he woke up the following day at noon, he was quite taken aback. His head, arms, and legs were in bandages. Hovering by his bedside were his crying wife and a doctor with a worried look on his face.

FEAST-DAY GRATUITIES

(From the Notebook of a Provincial Scrounger)

I list the donors one by one:

House No. 113. At apartment number 2, we came upon an individual of some education, who was quite well-intentioned to all appearances, if somewhat peculiar. Handing us our feast-day gratuity, he said: "Being a man of means, I am happy to offer this gratuity, but being at the same time a man of science who is accustomed to understanding objects and actions by studying their roots and causes, I would like to ask if there is a moral law by which you go from house to house collecting holiday gratuities, or if there is no such law and you are acting *à vol d'oiseau?*"*

As I espied in this question a thirst for knowledge, I sat down at his table that was decked with tasty morsels, and

---

* A comical misuse of the French term for "as the crow flies." [Translator]

offered the following explanation: "Gratitude is a quality inherent in lofty and noble souls. It is a quality intrinsic in man, and it is our duty to further it in every way possible among the people of this town, and not to let it die. A townsman who gives feast-day gratuities is, accordingly, exercising the beneficence of gratitude. It is in fact our duty to train you without respite in this sense of gratitude—on weekdays as well as feast days. But since, in addition to collecting gratuities, we have so many other responsibilities, the townsfolk must settle for a few days in the year for this training, in the hope that in the future, as human relations develop, gratuities will be proffered on a daily basis."

House No. 114. The owner, a Mr. Schweyn, gave me ten rubles with a sugary smile and a hearty handshake. One can only surmise that the old rogue has a messy backyard, or that he has someone living in the house illegally.

House No. 115. Madame Perechudova, the wife of the titular counselor, was put out when I entered her drawing room in my dirty galoshes. (Incidentally, she gave me three rubles.) Her lodger, Bryukhansky, when I requested that he fulfill his civic duty, refused so to do owing to a lack of funds. I explained to him: "On the evening of a feast day every townsman, before undertaking his usual expenditures on small luxuries, must weigh how much he will give and to whom, after consulting with the members of his family. He then divides the money depending on the number of recipients. If he has no money, he secures a loan; if for some reason he cannot secure a loan, he gathers his family and flees to Egypt . . . I wonder, sir, that you can even speak to me!" (I made note of his name.)

House No. 116. General Brindin, living in apartment number 3, proffering us five rubles said: "In my day I waged a battle against this evil, but for naught. The collecting of feast-day gratuities by toadies such as you is an insuperable evil! Here, take this and go to hell!"

A great general—but what a strange notion of civic duty.

MAY DAY AT SOKOLNIKI

The first of May was tending toward evening. The din of carriages, voices, and music drowned out the singing of birds and the whispering fir trees of Sokolniki. The feast was in full swing. A couple was sitting at one of the tea tables of the Staraya Gulyania, the gentleman in a shining top hat and the lady in a blue bonnet. On the table in front of them was a boiling samovar, an empty vodka bottle, cups, glasses, sliced sausages, orange peels, and such. The man was exceedingly drunk. He was staring intently at an orange peel, a vacant smile on his face.

"You're drunk as a skunk!" the lady mumbled angrily, looking about her nervously. "Drinking yourself under the table! It's not enough that everyone has to look away, but you're not having any fun yourself! Here you are with your cup of tea, and what does it taste like? You could be stuffing your mouth with marmalade or sausages—not that you'd know the difference! And to think I went to the trouble of ordering the best of everything!"

The vacant smile on the gentleman's face turned into an expression of great sorrow.

"M-Masha, where are they taking all these people?"

"Nowhere! They're just strolling about!"

"What about that policeman?"

"The policeman? He's just keeping an eye on things—maybe he's strolling about too! You're so drunk you don't know your right hand from your left!"

"I . . . I'm just . . . I'm an artist . . . a genre painter!"

"Drunk as a skunk! You should hold your tongue! Think before you start spouting rubbish! All around you there's grass, trees, shrubs, little twittering birds, and you see nothing, as if you weren't even here! You might as well be staring into the fog. A painter at least shows some interest in nature, and you? Drunk as a skunk!"

"Nature," the man says, looking around. "Nate-nature . . . birds singing . . . crocodiles crawling . . . lions . . . tigers . . ."

"Good heavens! Everyone is so proper, walking arm in arm, enjoying the music—and here you are making a spectacle of yourself! How did you get drunk so fast? One can't look away for a minute!"

"M-Masha," the man in the top hat muttered, turning white. "Quick . . ."

"Now what?"

"I want to go home . . . quick . . ."

"I'm sorry, you'll have to wait. We'll leave after dark. It's simply too embarrassing to have you stumbling all over the place, making a fool of yourself. Just sit there quietly and wait."

"I . . . I want to go home!"

He jumped up and, tottering, left the table. The people at nearby tables laughed out loud. The lady was mortified. "May God strike me down if I'm seen in public with you again!" she murmured, propping him up. "The shame of it! You're not even my husband—it's not like I have a ring or anything!"

"M-Masha, where are we?"

"Oh be quiet! Everyone's looking! This might be fine and dandy for you, but what about me? You're not even my husband—you give me a ruble, and then all I hear is 'I'm feeding you! I'm supporting you!' I spit on your money! As if I needed it! I'm going back to Pavel Ivanich!"

"M-Masha . . . I want to go home. Call a cab."

"All right then! But walk down that lane *in a straight line*, and I'll walk a little ways back. I can't afford to be seen with you in this state. *In a straight line!*"

The lady points the man who is *not even her husband* toward the exit and gives him a slight push. He moves forward quickly, tottering, bumping into people and chairs. The lady walks some distance behind him, watching him carefully. She is mortified and on edge.

"Walking sticks, fine walking sticks!" a man with a bundle of sticks and canes called out to the gentleman. "First-rate walking sticks, hickory, bamboo!"

The gentleman looked foolishly at the peddler and turned back, stumbling in the opposite direction, an expression of horror on his face.

"Where in heaven's name do you think you're going?" the lady said, grabbing him by the sleeve. "Tell me, where?"

"Where is Masha? M-Masha's gone . . ."

"And who am I, if not Masha?"

The lady took the gentleman under the arm and led him toward the exit. She was embarrassed.

"May God strike me down if I will ever be seen in public with you again," she mumbled, her face flushed with shame. "This is the last time I will put up with a spectacle of this kind. May God punish me . . . tomorrow I'm going straight back to Pavel Ivanich!" The lady raised her eyes timidly to the people all around, expecting to be met with mocking laughter. But all she saw were drunken faces, nodding heads, and stumbling revelers.

She was relieved.

THE MARRIAGE SEASON

(From the Notebook of a Marriage Broker)

Ivan Savvich Accumulatoff, provincial secretary, forty-two. Unsightly, pockmarked, voice gratingly nasal, yet all in all a fine figure of a man. Frequents all the best drawing rooms and the general's wife is his aunt. Lives from usury and is a crook, but is otherwise a decent enough fellow. Is seeking a young lady between eighteen and twenty, from a good home, and who knows French. Good looks are a must, as is a dowry of fifteen to twenty thousand rubles.

Prepossessoff, retired officer. A drinker prone to rheumatism. Is seeking a wife who will nurse him. Not averse to a widow (though not over the age of twenty-five). Must have capital.

Proudhonoff, photographic retoucher, seeks from photograph a bride who is not mortgaged, and will bring in at least two thousand a year. He drinks (not persistently, but with gusto), has brown hair, black eyes.

Madame Gnatskaya, widow. Has two houses and eleven hundred in cash. Seeks army general (even retired, if need be). Has a cataract in her left eye, though it is barely noticeable, and speaks with a whistle. Claims that although she is a widow she is in fact a virgin, as on her wedding night her late-lamented husband was overcome by palsy.

Diphtherit Alekseyich Mademoiselloff, thespian, thirty-five, of undetermined means. Claims his father owns a distillery (most certainly a tall tale). Invariably sports a coat and tails and a white cravat, as those are the only items of clothing he owns. Left the stage due to hoarseness of voice. Seeks merchant's daughter or widow of any shape or size, as long as she has money.

Plumpovsky, former staff captain, sentenced to exile in Siberia (Tomsk Province) for embezzlement and forgery. Wishes to make happy a poor orphan girl who would be prepared to follow him to Siberia. She must, however, be of noble lineage.

LETTERS TO THE EDITOR

I.

An Open Letter to Mr. Okrets

Dear Sir,

I have obliged your request to recommend your magazine *Luch* to friends and acquaintances; but as everyone I know lives quite far away, I have had to deliver your esteemed magazine to them with cabs or to recommend it to them by way of the municipal post. Consequently, I have spent eight rubles and eighty-five kopecks on said cabs and stamps. In the conviction that you

will be enough of a gentleman to send me
this sum at your earliest convenience,

I remain faithfully, etc.
R. Smirnov

The Town of Zhizdra, at Madame Khilkina's
residence

II.

An Open Letter to a Number of People

I am markedly popular. I may never have
raised a sword on a field of battle, or blown
up armored ships, or invented telephones,
but nevertheless I seem for some reason to
be blessed with some fame in Petersburg,
Moscow, and even Hamburg. In little or no
time I have received a flurry of invitations
and letters from the following esteemed per-
sonages and institutions: the banking offices
of Klim, the Hamburg Municipal Lottery,
the St. Petersburg school manual outlet,
five advertisements from the magazine *Nov*
and five from *Zhivopisnoe Obozreniye*, a
letter from Monsieur Leukhin's editorial
office, and from Ilin Maps and Charts, to

name a few. I am puzzled as to how they came to know me and my address. I would like herewith to express my gratitude to the aforementioned individuals and institutions for their flattering attention, but would ask them to desist from this uninterrupted constant correspondence, as it causes me a great inconvenience: postmen have tugged the cord of my doorbell to shreds, and the onslaught of letters has caused my neighbors, not to mention the keepers of the peace, puzzlement, doubts, and raised eyebrows in regard to my views.

III.

Letter to the Editor of Oskolki *Magazine*

Dear Sir,

One invariably hears complaints of how we have not kept up with the times, how Russia is lagging behind Western Europe. And indeed we are lagging behind by as much as twelve days! And yet it would be so easy for our Russian calendar to catch up: all we would have to do would be to count the first day of the year not as the first of January, but as the thirteenth.

Then we would stand shoulder to shoulder with all of Europe! I cannot perceive the slightest hitch in this. Except perhaps that ladies and maidens would suddenly find themselves twelve days older. But civil servants would be delighted: their salaries would be paid out much sooner. Of course, for those among us who are superstitious, it would be terrible to begin the year on the thirteenth. But must civilization bow and curtsy to superstitions? The mere thought of it! If we catch up with the rest of the world, we might even get ourselves a better rate of exchange.

Accept, my dear sir, etc.
Subscriber No. 11378

IV.

To the Editor of Raduga

Being a staunch aficionado of the performing arts, as is my daughter Zinaida, I herewith have the honor of requesting of the highly esteemed Monsieur Mansfeld that he pen for our private domestic use four comedies, three dramas, and two tragedies à la *Hamlet*, on the completion of which I will send you a three-ruble bill. (You may send me the change in postage stamps.) I herewith also consider it my duty to add that my neighbors who have ordered Monsieur Mansfeld's works either wholesale or retail are most satisfied, and are grateful at how cheap they are. We all also have the highest praise for Monsieur Mettsel for his kindness: on noting that the magazine *Raduga* could not accommodate all of Monsieur Mansfeld's works, he launched the magazine *Epokha* exclusively for them. What kindness!

Accept, dear sir, my humblest, and so on.
Colonel Kochkarev
Penza, on the second of January

VISITING CARDS

efore me on the table lie the visiting cards
with which my dear acquaintances have
graced me for the New Year. They send them so that the
postman can wear out his new shoes and doff his cap at my
maid. As an ancient philosopher once said: "Tell me who
sends you his visiting card, and I will tell you with whom
you are acquainted." Should anyone be interested in *my*
acquaintances, these are their cards:

An earl's coronet. Beneath it letters that smack of both
Gothic and the provincial: "Citoyen d'honneur, Klim
Ivanovich Deludedsky."

A visiting card with a golden border and a folded corner:
"Jean Pifficoff." This *Jean* is a hulking fellow with a hoarse
bass voice who exudes an aroma of vinegar, and roams the
earth in search of someone who has an ounce of pity for a
man fate has not been kind to, who has a ruble to lend him,
and who will offer him a glass of vodka.

Court Councilor and Chevalier, Dioscur Hemor-rhoidovich Lodkin.

Savaty Candelabrovich Buzzer-Wanderoffsky, Member of the Society for the Prevention of Cruelty to Animals, Agent of the Salamandra Fire Insurance Company, Roving Reporter for *Volna*, and Sales Representative for Singer & Co. sewing machines, etc.

Monsieur Franz Emilievich Pudique, Instructor in Social Dances and French Conversation.

Priestly Monk, Father Jeremiah.

A prince's coronet. Valentin Sisoyevich Sheet-Ofpaperoff, high school student.

A nondescript coronet. State Councilor Erast Crinolinovich Headlongoff.

Prince Agop Minayevich Obshiavishvili, Crimean and Georgian Wines and Spirits.

Also cards from, among others: Barrister's assistant Mitrofan Alexeyevich Bright-Redovich, Dysenteria Alexandrovna Imensova, Nikita Spevsipovich Runoff . . . Deacon Pyotr Ourdailybreadsky . . . Ivan Ivanich Diabolikoff, Editorial Assistant, *Rebus* Magazine . . . Antisemite Antisemitovich Okrets, Editor in Chief, *Luch* Magazine.

THE FOOLISH FRENCHMAN

Henri Pourquoi, a clown in the Gintz Brothers Circus, went into Moscow's renowned Testov Tavern to eat lunch.

"I'd like some consommé, please," he told the waiter.

"With poached eggs, or without?"

"Without—poached eggs might be a little too heavy for me. But I wouldn't mind two or three slices of toast."

While Pourquoi waited for his consommé, he looked around. The first thing he noticed was a portly gentleman at the next table, who was about to eat some blinis.

"My goodness," the clown muttered to himself as he watched his neighbor pour melted butter over the blinis. "The portions they serve in these Russian restaurants! Five blinis! Can one man eat so many?"

His neighbor was now heaping caviar onto the blinis. He cut them into halves, and had eaten them all within a minute.

"Hey there!" the man called out to the waiter. "I'll have another portion! Do you call these servings? You know what? Bring me ten, fifteen blinis right away! And a nice slice of sturgeon while you're at it, and some salmon!"

"How very odd," Pourquoi thought, peering at his neighbor. "He's just eaten five whole blinis and now he's ordering more! Not that this is a unique phenomenon. After all, Oncle François back in Brittany had no trouble downing two bowls of soup and five lamb chops at a single sitting. I've heard say that there are illnesses where people simply can't stop eating."

The waiter placed a platter piled with blinis and two plates before the clown's neighbor, one with sturgeon filets, the other with salmon. The portly gentleman drank a glass of vodka, ate a slice of salmon, and then turned his attention to the blinis. To the clown's amazement, he set about eating them like a starving man, barely pausing to chew.

"He's obviously sick," Pourquoi mused. "But does the poor misguided fool really think he can finish off that enormous pile of pancakes? Three more bites and his stomach will be full, but he'll still have to pay for the whole lot!"

"More caviar!" his neighbor called out, dabbing his oily lips with his napkin. "And don't forget the green onions!"

"But . . . half the pile is gone already!" the clown muttered to himself in horror. "My God! Has he already finished the whole plate of salmon? That isn't natural! Can a human stomach expand to such an extent? Impossible! It cannot expand beyond the belly! Back in France, exhibiting this man at a freak show you could rake in a fortune! Good heavens! The whole pile of blinis is gone!"

"And I'll have a bottle of Château Neuille," his neighbor said to the waiter, who had just brought him onions and more caviar. "But see that it's not overchilled! Hmm, what else do I want? Oh yes, another serving of blinis! But don't take all day!"

"Yes sir! And what will you be having as a second course?"

"Something lighter, I think. Get me a portion of sturgeon stew *à la russe*, will you? And also . . . um . . . give me a few minutes to think—off you go!"

"I must be dreaming!" the clown gasped, slumping against the back of his chair. "This man is courting death. No one can eat such a pile of food and expect to get away with it! Goodness! He's trying to commit suicide! It's written all over his sad face! But hasn't the waiter suspected anything? He must have!"

Pourquoi motioned to the waiter who had been serving his neighbor, and asked him in a whisper: "Why are you giving him so much food?"

"Well, the gentleman ordered it. What am I supposed to do," the waiter asked in surprise, "not serve him?"

"But he might keep ordering food all day and all night! If you don't have the pluck to stop him, then get the manager to, or call the police!"

The waiter grinned, shrugged his shoulders, and walked away.

"Barbarians!" the Frenchman uttered indignantly. "They are delighted that a madman, a suicidal maniac, is sitting here spending his rubles on their food! They don't care that this man is eating himself to death as long as the money keeps rolling in!"

"I don't think much of the service here!" the portly gentleman growled, turning to the Frenchman. "I can't tell you how all this waiting irritates me! They make you wait a good half hour from one plate to the next! No wonder your appetite goes to the dogs! Not to mention that they make you late—it's three o'clock already, and I'm expected at an anniversary dinner at five!"

"Pardon, monsieur," Pourquoi said, his face ashen, "but you are already dining!"

"No-o-o! You call this dining? This is lunch—a few little blinis."

The waiter placed the stew in front of the portly gentleman, who filled his plate, sprinkled cayenne pepper over it, and began slurping down one spoonful after another.

"The poor man," the French clown muttered, appalled. "He is either sick, or simply not aware of the danger he is in—or he is doing this on purpose . . . with the intention of committing suicide! Lord in heaven! Had I known what my eyes would see in this place, nothing on earth would have induced me to come here! My nerves aren't strong enough for such a spectacle!"

The Frenchman looked pityingly at his neighbor, waiting from minute to minute for the convulsions to begin, the same convulsions that had invariably gripped Oncle François after his dangerous meals.

"It's plain to see that the man is intelligent, young, and full of vitality," Pourquoi thought, eyeing his neighbor. "He might serve his country well, and it wouldn't surprise me in the least if he has a young wife too, and children. And judging by his clothes he must be well-to-do, with a good position. But what could push a man like that to such drastic measures? Couldn't he have chosen another way of doing himself in? It's amazing how little life is valued! How low and contemptible I am, sitting here without offering him a helping hand! Perhaps he can still be saved!"

Pourquoi resolutely got up from his chair and walked over to his neighbor.

"Excuse me, monsieur," he said in a hushed, ingratiating voice. "Though I have not had the honor of being introduced to you, I would like to assure you that you can think of me as a friend. Can I be of help to you in any way? Don't forget that you are still young . . . that you have a wife, children."

"I don't know what you're talking about!" the man said, glaring at the Frenchman.

"Let us not mince words at a time like this, monsieur! After all, I have eyes in my head! You are eating so much, that I . . . can but conjecture—"

"Me? Eating so much?" the man spluttered. "Me? Come, come! I haven't had a bite to eat since breakfast!"

"But you are eating incredible amounts of food!"

"What are you worried about? It's not as if you have to foot the bill! And what makes you think that I am eating all that much? Look around you!—I'm not eating more than anyone else!"

Pourquoi looked around, and tottered. Waiters bustling past each other were carrying plates piled high with food. The tables were filled with people devouring mountains of blinis, salmon, and caviar with as much gusto as the portly gentleman.

"O strange and wild country!" the French clown thought as he left the restaurant. "Not only is your climate miraculous, but so are the bellies of your people! O wondrous Russia!"

PERSONS ENTITLED TO TRAVEL FREE OF CHARGE ON THE IMPERIAL RUSSIAN RAILWAYS

IN FIRST-CLASS CARRIAGES

1) All railroad employees, without exception, their assistants, their lady assistants, and their assistants' assistants.
Note: Lower-ranking railway workers with grimy faces and dirty overalls (such as oilmen and depot workers) do not have the right to travel free of charge.

2) The wives of railway employees, their parents, children, grandchildren, great-grandchildren, sisters-in-law, sisters, brothers, mothers-in-law, aunts, parents of godchildren, godparents, godchildren, cousins, nephews, in fact relatives of every rank and classification, nannies, maids, as well as mistresses and gentlemen friends.

3) Station buffet attendants, their wives and acquaintances.

4) Landowners of the area traveling to a station in order to play a game of whist with the stationmaster, their wives, and relatives.

5) Guests of railroad employees.
   Note: In cases where drawn-out goodbyes are called for, the stationmaster may delay the train for up to twenty minutes.

6) All acquaintances of the conductor, without exception.

7) All creditors of the Imperial Russian Railways.

IN SECOND-CLASS CARRIAGES

1) Valets of railroad employees, cooks, scullery maids, coachmen, housemaids, and chimney sweeps.

2) The servants of the relatives and acquaintances of railroad employees.

3) The relatives and acquaintances of the servants of railroad employees.

4) Horses, donkeys, and oxen in the service of the railroads.

IN THIRD-CLASS CARRIAGES

1) All passengers who have purchased tickets for first- or second-class carriages, but cannot secure a place as said carriages are filled with passengers traveling for free.
Note: The aforementioned ticketed passengers may travel in third-class carriages standing. The board of the Libau-Romensk Railway Line will also permit them to lie beneath the benches or hang from coat hooks.

THE PROPOSAL

(A Tale for Young Ladies)

Valentin Petrovich Perederkin, a young man of pleasant demeanor, put on his coat and tails, slipped into lacquered pointed boots, donned a top hat, and, struggling to contain his agitation, drove to Princess Vera Zapiskina's estate.

What a pity, gentle reader, that you are not acquainted with the princess! What a sweet and charming creature she is: soft eyes the color of the sky, locks silken and wavy! The waves of the sea may break upon the rocky shore, but on the waves of the princess's locks every stone crumbles to dust. Only an undiscerning dunce can remain unmoved by her smiles and the warmth emanating from her miniature bust that seems chiseled from the finest stone. Only a hard-boiled brute will not be transported to the heights of bliss when she speaks, laughs, or shows her dazzlingly white teeth.

Perederkin was shown into the drawing room.

He took a seat opposite the princess.

"There is something, dearest princess," he began falteringly, "that I would like to ask you."

"I'm listening."

"Princess . . . forgive me, I do not know how to begin . . . you will surely find this so sudden . . . so impromptu . . . you will be angry."

He took a handkerchief from his pocket and wiped the sweat from his brow. The princess smiled and looked at him questioningly.

"From the moment I set eyes on you," he continued, "my heart . . . my heart was filled with a longing that leaves me no peace day or night! And if this longing is not assuaged, I . . . I will be very unhappy!"

The princess lowered her eyes pensively. Perederkin fell silent for a moment, but then continued. "You will surely be taken aback by what I have to say . . . you have such a lofty nature, far above mine, but in my eyes you are the ideal person for me."

Silence hung in the air. Perederkin sighed.

"And of course my estate does border on yours . . . and I am a man of considerable means."

"What is this about?" the princess asked demurely.

"What is this about?" Perederkin said heatedly, and rose. "Princess, I beg you, do not reject me! Do not destroy all my dreams! Dearest princess, I would like to make a proposal."

Perederkin sat down quickly, and leaned toward the princess. "A most profitable one, as you will see," he whispered. "In a single year we could sell a million *poods* of lard. I am proposing that we set up a lard processing factory on our estates, fifty-fifty."

The princess thought awhile. "Fifty-fifty?" she said. "It's a deal!"

And the innocent reader, who expected a melodramatic ending, can breathe a sigh of relief.

MAN

(A Few Philosophical Musings)

A tall, slender, dark-haired man—still young, though now approaching more mature years—stood at the door in his black frock coat and snow-white cravat, gazing sadly into the room filled with dazzling lights and waltzing couples.

"How dreary and hard is the life of man!" he mused. "Man is a slave not only to his passions but also to his fellow men. Yes, a slave! I am a slave to this bright and merry crowd, which pays me so it need not notice me. Its will, its slightest whim, shackles my hands and feet, its gaze crushes me like a python crushes a rabbit. I am not averse to toiling, I am happy to serve, but this subservience makes me ill! Why am I here? Whom am I serving? This eternal whirl, with its ladies and ice cream, its flowers and champagne, that knocks me off my feet! Unbearable! How terrible is the lot of man! How happy I will be when I cease to be one!"

It is uncertain to what depths the young pessimist's thoughts might have plummeted had not a young woman of remarkable beauty approached him. Her face was aglow, and exuded resolve. She ran her glove over her alabaster forehead, and, in a voice that sounded like music, said, "A glass of water, my good man!"

The good man put on a respectful face, and hurried off to fetch one.

FROM THE NOTEBOOK OF A COUNTRY SQUIRE

Upon his retirement, State Councilor Kaprikornov bought himself a small country estate on which he settled. There, in imitation partly of Cincinnatus, partly of the mushroom specialist Professor Kaigorodov, he toiled the land and recorded his observations on nature. After his death his notes, along with the rest of his property, was transferred by his last will and testament to his housekeeper, Marfa Evlampiyevna, a devoted old soul who had the manor house pulled down and a sturdy tavern that served liquor built in its place. This tavern had a special *clean* room for traveling landowners and officials, and on the table in that room she placed the deceased's bundle of notes, in case someone needed a piece of scrap paper. One of these pieces of paper has fallen into my hands; from what I could surmise, it must have been from the beginning of the deceased's agricultural notes, and contains the following entries:

March 3. The birds of spring are now arriving. Yesterday I saw some sparrows. Greetings to you, O children of southern climes! In your sweet chirping I believe I hear you calling back to me: "And a good day to you, Your Excellency!"

March 14. Today I asked Marfa Evlampiyevna: "Why does our cockerel crow so often?" Her answer: "Because he has a throat." So I said: "I, too, have a throat, and yet I do not crow!" Oh the mysteries of nature!

    All the years I served in St. Petersburg I often ate turkeys, but saw my first live one yesterday. A most remarkable bird.

March 22. The village constable came by. We had a long talk—I seated, he standing—about the virtues. As we conversed, he asked me: "If given the opportunity, Your Excellency, would you wish to be young again?" To which I replied: "No, I would not. If I were young again I would not have the high rank I have attained." He agreed with me, and, visibly moved, went on his way.

April 16. With my own hands I dug two vegetable beds in the garden and sowed semolina in them. I did not tell a soul about this, as I wanted the semolina beds to be a surprise for dear Marfa Evlampiyevna, to whom I owe so many happy moments. Yesterday, as we were having tea, she lamented the condition her figure was in, complaining that her size no longer allowed her to fit through the pantry door. I remarked to her: "On the contrary, my dearest, the fullness of your form frames you most wonderfully and fans my inclination." She blushed, and I stood up and embraced her with both arms (as one can no longer reach around her with just one).

May 28. An old man who saw me by the women's bathing place asked me why I was sitting there. To which I replied: "I am keeping watch to make sure that no young men approach." "Let us both keep watch," the old man said, and, sitting down next to me, we began to discuss the virtues.

NADIA N.'S VACATION HOMEWORK

Give five examples of relative clauses.

1) Not too long ago Rushia waged war on foreign parts, by the way killing many Turks

2) The railroad is screechy, carries people, and is maid of rails and materials.

3) Beef is maid of bulls and cows, while mutton is maid of sheep and baby lambs.

4) Papa was passed over for a medal, so he

got angry and retired due to domestic reasons.

5) I adore my friend Dunya Walk-on-Waters-kaya for her diligence and attention in class and for being skillful at introducing me to the hussar Nikolai Spiridonich.

Give five examples of word agreement.

1) During Lent, priests and men of the cloth refuse to marry newlyweds.

2) Peasants live in country houses both summer and winter, beat their horses, but are terribly unclean, for they are bespattered with tar and refuse to hire maids and porters.

3) Parents give their daughters to military men who have a fortune and their own house.

4) Young boy! You must honor your papa and your mama, and thus you will be a pretty child and loved by everyone in the world.

5) No chance had he for one last sigh, As the lunging bear did upon him fly.

COMPOSITION

How did you spend your vacation?

The instant I passed my examinations I left with Mama, our furniture, and my brother

Ioanni, a third-year lycée student, for our summer dacha. We were visited by: Katya Kuzevich with her mama and papa, Zina, little Egor, Natasha, and many other friends of mine, who took walks with me and embroidered out of doors. There were a lot of men, but us maidens kept away from them and paid no attention to them whatsoever. I read many books, among them Meshchersky, Maikov, Dumas, Livanov, Turgenev, and Lomonosov. Nature was at its zenith, the young trees growing in rampant profusion, no ax having yet sought out their robust trunks, and the delicate foliage cast a breezy, all-engulfing shade over the reedy soft grasses speckled with the gilded tips of buttercups, an azure spray of bluebells, and crimson cloves. (Teacher's note: evidently lifted from Turgenev's "Silent Moment"!) The sun rose and it set. Where it rose there was a herd of birds flying. There was this shepherd who was shepherding his sheep, and there were some clouds floating under the sky. Oh how I do love nature! My papa was jittery all summer long. The evil bank wanted to take possession of our house just like that, and Mama never left Papa's side as she was afraid he would take his own life. I had a very good vacation because I studied science and comported myself very well. The end.

ARITHMETIC

Three merchants invested capital in a trading enterprise, which within a year brought them a profit of 8,000 rubles. Question: How much did each receive if the first merchant invested 35,000 rubles, the second 50,000, and the third 70,000?

> Answer: To solve the problem, one has to begin by figuring out which of the merchants invested the most money. This can be done by taking the three amounts and subtracting them from one another, from which we see that the third merchant invested most, as he did not invest 35,000, or 50,000, but 70,000. Fine. The next step is figuring out how much each of the merchants received, for which we must divide 8,000 into three parts so that the largest part will go to the third merchant. Division: three goes into eight two times. 3 x 2 = 6. Fine. Subtract six from eight which leaves you with 2. Add a zero. Subtract eighteen from twenty which again leaves you with two. Keep adding zeros till the end. The result is 2 rubles and 666 and 2/3 kopecks, which leads us to deduce that each merchant should have received 2 rubles and 666 and 2/3 kopecks, and the third merchant a little bit more.

Authenticated by—Chekhonte

WORDS, WORDS, WORDS

Gruzdev, a young telegraph operator, was lounging on a sofa in a hotel room, his light-blond head propped on his hands. He was gazing at a tiny red-haired young woman.

"Tell me, Katya, what led you to become a fallen woman?" he asked with an offhand sigh. "By the way, you look frozen through!"

It was one of the worst possible March nights. The dull flicker of the streetlamps barely lit the grimy, thinning snow. Everything was wet, dirty, and gray. The wind moaned quietly, timidly, as if afraid it might be forbidden to sing. There was the sound of heavy feet tramping through the slush. Nature was in the grip of nausea.

"What led you to become a fallen woman?" Gruzdev asked again.

Katya looked shyly into his eyes. They were honest,

warm, sincere eyes, she thought. Fallen creatures are drawn to honest eyes like moths to a flame. A kind look is worth more than a full bowl of gruel. Embarrassed, picking at the fringe of the tablecloth, she told Gruzdev her sad tale. A humdrum tawdry tale: a man, promises, deceit, and so on.

"What a scoundrel!" Gruzdev muttered indignantly. "Brutes like that should be rounded up and sent to hell one and all! Was he rich?"

"Yes."

"I knew it! But you women are just as much to blame, hankering after money like that! What do you need all that money for?"

"He swore he would take care of me for the rest of my life," Katya whispered. "Is that so bad? How could I resist? I have a poor old mother to care for!"

"What unfortunate creatures you are! And you all end up like this out of sheer foolishness, out of idiocy! You women are all so fainthearted! Unfortunate, pitiful! Listen, Katya! It's none of my business, and I'm the last person to want to meddle in other people's affairs, but your face is so sad I have to speak my mind! Why don't you return to a respectable life? Aren't you ashamed of yourself? After all, it's plain to see that you are not completely ruined yet, that you can still turn back! Why don't you at least try to be respectable again? You could, Katya, I'm sure of it! You have an honest face, and in your eyes there is goodness, sorrow. You have such a nice smile!"

Gruzdev took Katya by both hands and, looking through her eyes into her soul, uttered many kind words. He spoke in a soft trembling tenor, his eyes filled with tears. His hot breath poured over her face and neck.

"You can be respectable again, Katya! You are still young, you must try!"

"I have tried, but . . . but nothing came of it! I tried everything! Once I even started working as a scullery maid, though . . . though I am of noble lineage! I wanted to give up my life of sin! Better the dirtiest drudgery than the trade I am in now! I worked as a scullery maid in a merchant's house. I stayed there for a month and I made do, life was livable. But the mistress was a jealous woman, even though I never paid the slightest attention to the master. Finally she threw me out, and again I had nowhere to go, and . . . and I ended up where I started! Right where I started!"

Katya's eyes widened, her face grew pale, and suddenly she let out a shriek. In the room next door something fell crashing to the floor—Katya's shriek must have startled someone. Her thin hysterical sobs echoed through the flimsy partition between the rooms. Gruzdev quickly got her some water. Ten minutes later Katya was lying on the sofa, still sobbing, "What a worthless woman I am! The worst in the whole world! I will never manage to return to a life of decency now! Never! I will never manage to lead a virtuous life! How can I? I am so vile! I am so ashamed! But I deserve no better!"

Katya said little, not as much as Gruzdev, but there was candor in her words. She wanted to make a full confession, the confession of an honest sinner, but her words did not amount to more than moral self-flagellation. Again and again she clawed at her soul.

"I have tried and tried, but nothing ever comes of it! Nothing! I might as well perish!" she finally concluded with a sigh, and carefully set about rearranging her hair.

The young man looked at the clock.

"I will never amount to anything, but still, I am so grateful to you! This is the first time in my life that anybody has spoken such kind words to me. You are the only person who has ever treated me humanely, even though I am a vile, fallen woman!"

And suddenly she fell silent. A novel she had once read flashed through her mind. The hero had befriended a fallen woman and after much back and forth had convinced her to return to a life of virtue, and after she returned to a life of virtue he had made her his mistress. Katya thought awhile. Was not blond Gruzdev the hero of that novel? Was he not at least a little bit like him? Quite like him, she mused. With a pounding heart, she looked into his eyes. Tears ran in streams down her cheeks.

"There, there, Katya, calm down!" Gruzdev sighed, looking at the clock. "If you really want to, I'm sure you'll be able to turn your back on this life."

Katya, still crying, slowly unbuttoned the three top buttons of her coat. The novel with the eloquent hero faded from her mind.

The distraught wind howled through the ventilation shaft as if it was the first time it had ever seen the violence human beings will submit to in quest of their daily bread. High up above, on another floor, someone was plucking at an untuned guitar. The most humdrum of music.

THE FRENCH BALL

"I want you to go to the French ball tonight. You're the only one I can think of sending. I want a full article—if possible even a story. The more detail the better. If for whatever reason you can't go, then let me know as soon as possible and I'll send someone else. I'll get you a ticket by seven.

(The editor's signature)

P.S. At the ball, buy yourself a raffle ticket—the office will pay. Good luck in winning the prize the president of the French Republic has sent. Is it true you're getting married?"

After reading this letter, Peter Semyonich, journalist, roving reporter, and humorist, lay down on the sofa, lit a cigarette, and patted his belly with self-satisfaction. (He had just eaten lunch, and was nursing a feeling akin to self-less, platonic love in the vicinity of his stomach.)

"At the ball, buy yourself a raffle ticket—the office will pay!" he mimicked the editor's letter. "What generosity! For the next two years I won't hear the end of it! The scoundrel! He's as tightfisted as Scrooge! He should see how editorial offices abroad work. They know how to value a man, they never scrimp and save! Say you are Stanley and about to set out in search of Livingston: Here's a few thousand pounds sterling for you! Say you're Mr. John Bull and about to set out in search of Janet: Here's ten thousand pounds for you! You are about to set out to write a piece on the French ball: Here's a thousand fifty for you! That's how it is abroad, and what do *I* get? A raffle ticket! He pays me five kopecks a line, and then he thinks that I . . . the scoundrel!"

Pyotr Semyonich closed his eyes and thought awhile. A multitude of thoughts big and small whirled through his head. But soon they were enveloped in a pleasant pinkish mist. A thick, opaque liquid slowly oozed through all the cracks, holes, and windows of the room. The ceiling began to descend. Little people and miniature horses with ducks' heads began swarming about; a large soft wing fanned out, a river flowed. A tiny typesetter carrying huge letters walked past with a grin, a grin that engulfed everything, and . . . Pyotr Semyonich sank into a dream.

He put on his coat and tails, his white gloves, and left the house. The carriage with the newspaper's insignia was already waiting. A coachman in livery jumps off the box and helps him into the soft velvet seat.

"This is all so inconvenient, dammit!" he thinks. "I can't even stretch my legs in here."

A few minutes later the carriage pulls up at the door of the Imperial Association of Nobles. Pyotr Semyonich frowns and hands the porter his coat. Slowly and with gravity, as befits his standing as a reporter, he climbs the ornate and brilliantly lit flight of stairs. What extravagance! Everything is just as the poster had proclaimed, only bigger and better. Tropical plants, flowers from Nice, a thousand costumes.

"It's the reporter!" a whisper runs through the crowd. "It's him!"

A little old man comes hurrying up to him with an anxious look on his face and a Légion d'honneur medal on his lapel.

"Forgive me!" he says to Pyotr Semyonich. "Please forgive me! Had we known that you were coming we would not have placed this palm tree here. This palm tree is too small and insignificant to have the right to stand in the presence of a journalist from a newspaper such as—"

"Enough, enough, my good man! You are unsettling me, enough!" And suddenly, to his own amazement, fluent French begins pouring from his lips. In the past, the only word he had known was *merci*—but now there was no holding him back. That just goes to prove that if you're not careful you'll be chattering away in Chinese before you know it!

So many people he knows are there. And every newspaperman! Linskerov walks by. Myasnitsky and Baron Galkin . . . Even Palmin is there. Yaron, Gerson, and Kicheyevich go by.

Shekhtel and Chekhov the painter urge him to buy some flowers.

"Can it be that your office is so poor that it can't afford to pay for a few flowers?" Baron Galkin asks him in amazement.

Pyotr Semyonich pays a hundred rubles for a flower, and at that very moment a messenger brings him a telegram from his editor: "See to it that you win the raffle prize sent by the president of the French Republic and describe your impressions. Wire back up to a thousand words. Money no object." He goes to the raffle stand and begins buying raffle tickets. He buys one . . . two . . . ten . . . a hundred—finally a thousand, and he does manage to win the Sèvres vase that is the prize. Hugging it in both arms, he walks on.

A lady with blue eyes and luxuriant flaxen hair comes toward him. Her gown, needless to say, is beyond compare. A crowd is following her.

"Who is that?" Pyotr Semyonich, enraptured, asks Myasnitsky.

"A renowned Frenchwoman. She was sent over from Nice along with the flowers."

Pyotr Semyonich walks up to her and introduces himself. Within a minute he has taken her by the arm, and they promenade at great length. There is a lot he needs to find out from her, a lot. She is so wonderful!

"But where will I put that vase in my room?" he wonders, his eyes brimming with admiration for the Frenchwoman. His room is small, and the vase keeps growing and growing until it has outgrown the room. He begins to weep. He cries bitter tears, like a woman mourning the sudden death of her husband.

"Aha! So you love that vase more than you love me?" the Frenchwoman suddenly shouts, and slams her fist against the vase. There is a loud crash, and the precious vase shatters on the floor. The Frenchwoman laughs out loud and runs off into the mists. All the newspapermen stand around laughing. Pyotr Semyonich, foaming at the mouth, charges at them, and, suddenly finding himself in the Bolshoi Theatre, tumbles over a railing and falls head-first from the sixth tier.

He opens his eyes and finds himself lying on the floor near his sofa.

"Thank God there's no Frenchwoman," he mutters to himself, rubbing his eyes. "That means the vase isn't broken . . . I mustn't get married, otherwise I'll have children, and they'll romp around and break the vase!"

He rubs his eyes again, but still cannot see the vase.

"It was all a dream," he realizes. "Ha! It's already midnight! The ball has been going on for quite a while. I'd better get going! Well . . . let me just rest for a few minutes, and then I'll go."

He rested for a few minutes, and fell asleep again.

"So?" the editor asked him the following day. "Did you go to the ball? Was it fun?"

"Nothing special," Pyotr Semyonich replied, handing the editor the piece he had written. "I was bored the whole time. Oh, and yes, I bought a raffle ticket, you owe me a ruble—don't forget."

The article was somewhat dry, but rather well-written.

About the Author

ANTON CHEKHOV (1860–1904) is regarded as one of the world's modern masters of both the play and the short story.

About the Translator

PETER CONSTANTINE'S recent translations include *The Essential Writings of Rousseau* (Modern Library), *The Essential Writings of Machiavelli* (Modern Library), Sophocles' *Theban Trilogy* (Barnes and Noble Classics), and works by Gogol, Dostoevsky, Tolstoy, and Voltaire. His translation of the complete works of Isaac Babel for W. W. Norton received the Koret Jewish Literature Award and a National Jewish Book Award citation. He has been a Guggenheim Fellow, and was awarded the PEN Translation Prize for *Six Early Stories* by Thomas Mann. He co-edited *A Century of Greek Poetry: 1900–2000*, and the anthology *The Greek Poets: Homer to the Present*, which W. W. Norton published in 2010. He is currently a fellow in Greek/Classics at Columbia.

About Seven Stories Press

SEVEN STORIES PRESS is an independent book publisher based in New York City. We publish works of the imagination by such writers as Nelson Algren, Russell Banks, Octavia E. Butler, Ani DiFranco, Assia Djebar, Ariel Dorfman, Coco Fusco, Barry Gifford, Martha Long, Luis Negrón, Hwang Sok-yong, Lee Stringer, and Kurt Vonnegut, to name a few, together with political titles by voices of conscience, including Subhankar Banerjee, the Boston Women's Health Collective, Noam Chomsky, Angela Y. Davis, Human Rights Watch, Derrick Jensen, Ralph Nader, Loretta Napoleoni, Gary Null, Greg Palast, Project Censored, Barbara Seaman, Alice Walker, Gary Webb, and Howard Zinn, among many others. Seven Stories Press believes publishers have a special responsibility to defend free speech and human rights, and to celebrate the gifts of the human imagination, wherever we can. In 2012 we launched Triangle Square books for young readers with strong social justice and narrative components, telling personal stories of courage and commitment. For additional information, visit www.sevenstories.com.